THE WIND ALONG THE RIVER

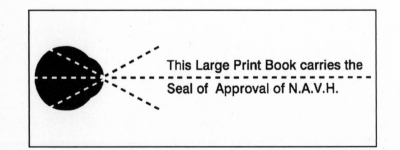

This Large Print Book carries the
Seal of Approval of N.A.V.H.

THE WIND ALONG THE RIVER

JACQUELYN COOK

THORNDIKE PRESS

A part of Gale, Cengage Learning

Detroit • New York • San Francisco • New Haven, Conn • Waterville, Maine • London

GALE
CENGAGE Learning™

Copyright © 1986 by Jacquelyn Cook.
The River Series #2.
Thorndike Press, a part of Gale, Cengage Learning.

Thorndike Press® Large Print Clean Reads.
The text of this Large Print edition is unabridged.
Other aspects of the book may vary from the original edition.
Set in 16 pt. Plantin.

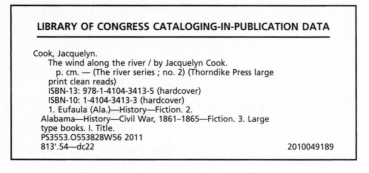

LIBRARY OF CONGRESS CATALOGING-IN-PUBLICATION DATA

Cook, Jacquelyn.
    The wind along the river / by Jacquelyn Cook.
        p. cm. — (The river series ; no. 2) (Thorndike Press large
    print clean reads)
    ISBN-13: 978-1-4104-3413-5 (hardcover)
    ISBN-10: 1-4104-3413-3 (hardcover)
    1. Eufaula (Ala.)—History—Fiction. 2.
    Alabama—History—Civil War, 1861–1865—Fiction. 3. Large
    type books. I. Title.
    PS3553.O553828W56 2011
    813'.54—dc22   2010049189

Published in 2011 by arrangement with BelleBooks, Inc.

Printed in the United States of America
1 2 3 4 5 6 7 15 14 13 12 11

A12005 678297

The Wind Along the River

CHAPTER 1

A sudden chill wind snatched Emma's cashmere shawl, threatening to fling it into the Chattahoochee far, far below. Engulfed in loneliness, she had stood too long on the bluff overlooking the river. Evening slipped silently around her, bringing an end to the December day, mild even for Alabama.

Shivering, Emma Edwards glanced at the lowering sky and sighed. She must hurry home to Barbour Hall because her sister-in-law, Cordelia, who thought Emma's only purpose in life was to obey her whims, would be angry again. Lily always said God had a plan for everyone, but Emma thought He had not noticed her. Love had passed her by. At twenty-seven, she had reached the evening of her life.

Blat! Blat! A sharp sound echoed from the hills behind her, seemingly a part of her exploding emotions. Her spreading skirt, weighed down by hoops, and her honey-colored hair, drawn back into a tight knot at the back of her slender neck, remained unruffled by the wind. Her delicate fingers smoothed the lines of her cheeks into an expression as placid as the distant water. She would not allow herself another sigh or frown; but as her gaze dropped to the riverbank at the base of the bluff and to the waves rolling into the shore, lapping, churning, whipping into a white froth, she could feel the same restlessness pounding ceaselessly within her. Surely December 20, 1860, would be a date forever seared upon her brain.

The sun had set behind Eufaula, yet the many mansions of the city sparkled as if their windows were studded with diamonds. They wavered before her startled blue eyes in a haze she knew to be smoke because her throat burned from her sudden gasp. Echoing reports of discharging cannon again assaulted her ears. Squinting to focus the blurred scene, she was able to discern, etched against a blazing bonfire, a buggy rattling down the hill toward her.

"Emma, Emma, come quickly," Lily Wingate's lilting voice called. Her brown hair had slipped from its combs and was streaming in the wind. "Hurry! You mustn't miss the fun of the illuminations!"

"The what?" Emma's relieved laughter bubbled in her throat as she easily negotiated her willowy body into the red leather seat of the runabout. Suppressing her initial reaction of fear, she allowed her heart to respond, as always, with delight to the animation of her niece, just seven years her junior.

"Oh, it's all just too exciting," exclaimed Lily. "Didn't you hear the cannon signaling?"

"Of course," Emma answered.

"The tide can no longer be stemmed!" Lily's voice was shrill with fervor. "Since South Carolina has taken the irrevocable action of secession, the news is coming in that all over the South people are joining in illumination night!"

The buggy swayed as they crossed Randolph Avenue, and Lily struggled with the reins. The horse threatened to rear as the people poured into the street, shouting, waving handkerchiefs. A brigade of soldiers, the Eufaula Rifles, marched smartly around the corner, accompanied by a drum's tattoo.

Emma could not seem to share Lily's exhilaration. As a spinster, she had no real place in Eufaula's kingdom of cotton. While she could sympathize with the local demand for states' rights and a low tariff so that the South could trade its cotton for cheap foreign goods, she had no voice of her own. From this beautiful city, located on a bluff one hundred and fifty feet above the Chattahoochee River separating Alabama from Georgia, cotton was taken on flat-bottomed side-wheelers down to Apalachicola, Florida, and thence to New York and Liverpool. She could easily understand why Eufaula's flourishing economy was based on land, cotton, and slaves; however, she existed only at the beneficence of her late brother, Clare Edwards. Her sister-in-law kept her in a nebulous position — below the other family members but slightly above the servants. Sometimes, only Lily's insistence that Emma had been granted a special gift kept her head erect, her lips smiling, and her heart searching.

Looking at vivacious Lily, Emma wished that she could share Lily's faith and confidence in her own ability to face whatever life brought.

For the last month, the townspeople had been holding their breaths, suspended, waiting for the weight to drop. Immediately after Lincoln's election in November, Barbour County had organized the Minutemen and called for secession and preparations for safety and resistance. Alabama had waited — to see what South Carolina would do. Eufaula's matrons had busily prepared for parties even while the convention deliberated. Drifting on the eddies of the group, Emma had not felt a part of the celebration.

Since noon today, when the news had spread like leaping flames from the Eufaula telegraph office that South Carolina was withdrawing from the nation, flags had been fluttering and young people had been popping firecrackers. Emma had withdrawn from the bustling excitement, feeling acutely that everyone was converging with a plan except her. Now as she looked at Lily, she stiffened her spine against the buggy seat and pulled her old canezou, a dainty jacket with horizontal rows of smocking, more closely around her neck. Shivering, glad she had brought the warm shawl, she wondered whether her chill came from night air or from her unreasonable premonition of fear.

Deftly controlling the horse, Lily pulled away from the crowd proceeding up the hill, gathering around Mayor Thornton's house for speeches. Though it was to be expected that their neighbor, Lewis Llewellen Cato, a member of the Eufaula Regency, would be entertaining a large crowd, Emma was surprised to see Barbour Hall ablaze with lights. It had not been so since Lily's father's death last year.

As they drove past the red cedars at the gates, Emma looked up at the magnificent white-frame mansion. Built in 1854 and considered one of the finest examples of Italianate architecture in the South, its floor-to-ceiling windows on both floors and in the belvedere crowning the roof were, every one, sparkling with light.

Lily giggled in delight. "The house looks dressed for a ball. Haven't I always said the glassed belvedere is her airy hat; the wooden balustrade, her neck ruffle; the green shutters on the upper story, her canezou, the porch spreading around the first floor, her hooped skirt — ?"

"And the trim for her skirt, the pairs of slender columns interspersed with lacy scrolls," Emma finished for her, laughing.

As the merry pair entered through the double doors, Lily's husband, Harrison Wingate, strode across the entry hall floor, a checkerboard of twelve-inch squares of black-and-white Italian marble. His smooth face brightened with a smile that lifted his mustache and radiated from his eyes as he greeted them. "As soon as I put this candlestand by the parlor window," he said, indicating the hand-carved mahogany *tor-chier* he carried, "and light one last candle, I'll be finished and ready to go. You're coming with us, Emma?"

"The house is already so bright, it could shine all the way to South Carolina," laughed Lily. Then she added emphatically, "Of course, she's coming. She stays alone in this house far too much. I'm not about to let her miss the most exciting thing that ever happened to Eufaula!"

Her face a mask, Emma looked toward the parlor. She dared not venture an answer until she sensed her sister-in-law's mood.

Cordelia Edwards was jovial. She sat close to the crackling fire that had been lighted beneath the mantel of white Italian marble. "Ah, boo, boo, boo," she laughed, jiggling her chins. The six-month-old baby, perched on Mrs. Edwards's stomach, rewarded her with a two-toothed grin. She looked up as the child's father brought in the waist-high stand, and her tone changed to icy sarcasm. "More candles, Captain Wingate? I really thought this room had quite enough light." She glanced meaningfully toward a multitude of candles lending fire to every crystal teardrop of the Waterford chandelier.

"This is the last one, Miss Cordelia," Harrison replied politely as he placed the *tor-*

13

chier so that the thick, tall candle would shine directly through the lace draperies on the huge square, six-over-six-pane windows. "The crowds are moving up the hill. We must give evidence of our support."

Lily crossed to her mother, dropped a kiss on her baby's dark fuzz of hair, and flopped on the double settee. Cocking her head to one side, she traced her finger over the elaborate Chippendale design of carved mahogany leaves and scrolls which formed the stiff back, and considered her mother before speaking. "Mama, do you feel like playing with Mignonne a little longer? We all wanted to attend the celebration on College Hill."

Emma sniffed in alarm. Lily had said "we." Emma had already been away from the house for more than an hour. Even though the clean, sharp smell of the oak wood fire invited her to warm her fingers, she had remained standing in the doorway, watching them obliquely in the huge, gold-leaf Belgian mirror over the mantel.

Mrs. Edwards frowned. "You girls know better than to be out about the town alone," she scolded, shaking her fingers until her black taffeta sleeves rustled.

"Yes, Ma'am," Lily replied meekly, "but this time Harrison will be with us."

14

"Perhaps I'd better stay and help keep . . . ," Emma interjected subserviently and hurried toward the fireside.

"Nonsense; I'll keep her. What are grand-mas for?" Cordelia Edwards bounced the baby for another grin. Mignonne watched with thick-lashed eyes, her apple cheeks waiting expectantly for reason to smile.

Quickly, Lily jumped to her feet and gave Emma a push. "Go put on something pretty," she commanded, then added under her breath, "Harrison has a friend I want you to meet."

Emma's cheeks, already as delicately hued as the inside of a seashell, lost all color, but she turned obediently into the hall and fled up the stairs.

In the blue and white room she had once shared with Lily, Emma hurriedly opened the walnut armoire in the back corner. Even though her brother had willed her a small income of her own, the huge wardrobe held only a few frocks. Excitedly, she fingered them with hands that shook at the thought her niece was matchmaking again.

Since Lily had married the riverboat captain two years ago, she seemed to think everyone should be as happily in love as she. But Emma had long ago resigned herself to spinsterhood; only occasionally did she let herself recall her long-ago love, at sixteen, the acceptable age for coming out in preparation for marriage. She had fallen in love with Michael, but her grandfather had refused permission for them to marry because the young man was not of their faith.

Shaking off her reverie with determination, she began to dress quickly. Dropping her daytime hoop, she stepped into a muslin petticoat run through with four steels from below the waist to the hem. The bottom hoop measured two-and-one-half yards around her feet and would keep her skirt extended fashionably. She decided to follow Lily's advice and wear her prettiest frock, a thick velvet in softly glowing pink. A wide band of ribbon and lace encrusted with crystals circled the slight train and rose in stairsteps in front to frame a cluster of crystal on watered silk roses in the center of the billowing skirt. A narrower band repeated the blocked design around the boat neckline and short, puffed sleeves.

Peering into the mirror over the marble-topped walnut dresser, she dusted a little whiting on her forehead and pinched her cheeks for color. Nothing she could do would keep her features from being plain; however, as she did with the rest of her life, she made the best of them. Fastening a necklace of crystals, she smiled. Lily would be pleased. Flinging on a wrap of pink moiré silk, quilted and lined with velvet, she started out, then ran back for her long, white kid gloves.

Glancing out the bedroom window, Emma saw a crowd of singing, shouting people surging up Barbour Street. They moved as if driven with a single sense of purpose. Pressing her hands against her chest, Emma swallowed convulsively. She had no purpose, no place with this moving throng. She leaned her head against the window frame. Maybe she should not intrude upon Lily and Harrison. She had been with them constantly before their marriage when she was needed as a chaperone; now, however, Lily continued to insist that she accompany them by saying that any situation was always smoothed by Emma's calm, pleasant manner.

A rueful laugh choked her. No one seemed to guess that her peacefulness was a sham. She kept her troubles in a tight little knot at the base of her throat and bravely tried to bear them alone. Looking down into the night, she wavered. Perhaps she should not go. She could stay in this room, her one refuge. No one entered here without her bidding — not even Cordelia.

Down below, flaming torches cast eerie shadows beneath the China trees, increasing her foreboding of something moving toward her. Her knees shook. Lily, who faced all of life like a great adventure, would laugh and chide her. Digging her fingernails into the curtains, Emma crushed the creamy lace in her clammy palm. Sparks from the *flambeaux* seemed to be pricking her soul. She breathed a long, steadying sigh. This was a celebration, a new beginning.

With trembling fingers, Emma smoothed her face into an enigmatic smile. She ran down the stairs and followed her family into the dark.

CHAPTER 2

The blaze of torches illuminated the happy faces of the crowd, thronging out from the Cato house next door and moving up Barbour Street. Emma was swept along as the mass surged across the block to Broad Street and the top of College Hill.

"Freedom from Northern oppressors!"

"Hurrah for a Southern Confederacy!"

Music, beating in stirring rhythm from the colonnaded portico of the Union Female College, spurred marching feet to assemble quickly. Emma noticed the local dignitaries — Judge John Gill Shorter, Edward Young, John McNab, Mayor Thornton, Colonel E. S. Shorter, and others, seated on the porch. With them were two strangers.

The younger man turned as Emma, Lily, and Harrison moved nearer. A smile danced over his even features as he singled them out of the crowd. Briefly saluting Captain Wingate, he continued to look their way.

He was staring at Lily, of course. Her marble-browed, raven-haired beauty was the current fashion rage; Emma's cool blondness was quite out of vogue.

Knowing she barely possessed the requisite handspan waist, Emma gave a self-derisive laugh that anyone would notice her. Loving Lily devotedly, gratefully, Emma felt no pangs of jealousy. Her only joy of living came through sharing Lily's family, and she had long ago resigned herself to the fact that her chance of having a life of her own was nearing an end. Sighing, she raised her chin with determination. Without volition, her lashes also lifted in response to the sensing of a stare. Startled, she met with sudden impact his dark and laughing eyes.

Blushing, she turned her attention to Professor J. C. Van Houten as he stood before a group of girls dressed in their brown merino school uniforms. The crimson ribbons on their brown hats quivered with their excitement as they lifted their high, sweet voices in patriotic songs, composed especially for the occasion by their beloved teacher.

Still feeling warm eyes upon her, Emma averted her gaze and tilted her chin. On the college roof she could see the slightly larger-than-life-sized statue of Minerva, goddess of wisdom, science, and the arts, determinedly clutching her wooden diploma. It always amused Emma that the lady's Roman garments had been exchanged for staid, high-necked, long-sleeved, full-skirted garb so that her carved cypress self looked exactly like the schoolgirls below, down to — no, up to — her hair, parted in the middle and fashioned into wooden, long curls at each side. Emma laughed in spite of herself.

The stranger was laughing with her! *Impudent fellow!* How dare he think she was responding to him? Her cheeks blazing, she edged behind Harrison Wingate's substantial back. From this obscurity, she let the impassioned words of John Gill Shorter, the first of the signers of the Minutemen, slide over her shoulders.

Emma looked up at Minerva. *You and I are the only ones not excited,* she thought. *Can anyone really think Lincoln will allow us to have our own nation and not make war?*

As the cheers and applause died down, Emma peered around Harrison's shoulder just as the words of another speaker — Jonathan Ramsey of Georgia, had been his introduction — made the crowd roar with laughter. His entire talk was laced with humor and predictions of how easily the

21

South would whip the North, if indeed the matter should come to war.

Blat! Blat! The twelve-pound Napoleon fired again. Emma jumped so hard her tense neck muscles hurt. The acrid smell of the black powder made her grimace. The cannon had signaled that the speeches were over. The roué from Georgia was shouldering his way through the crowd toward them.

Harrison gave him a congratulatory handshake and turned to the red-faced Emma. "May I present my dear friend and fellow sailor, Jonathan Ramsey from Bulloch County, Georgia."

Emma managed the proper polite bow and pleasant look required by a lady's introduction to a gentleman; however, she narrowed her eyes to convey reproving anger because of his liberties of familiarity. He bowed swiftly and brushed his mustache over her extended hand. "You must be the lovely Miss Emma." He lifted his head and spoke so exuberantly that his dark curls bounced. "Miss Lily does go on and on about you."

Laughing, unable to sustain anger as she looked into his twinkling eyes, Emma said fondly, "She does go on and on about everything."

"I'm as dry as a bone in the desert after

all that speechifying." Ramsey chuckled and clapped his hand against his bright cravat as if he were choking. "Let's make a round of the parties. I hear Colonel Chambers is serving eggnog — that is, unless you ladies are hostessing a party . . ." He lifted quizzical, black eyebrows and waited hopefully.

"Oh, no," Lily responded quickly. "We'd be delighted to accompany you tonight —" Her brown eyes darted a look at Emma, and she continued briskly, "but we are planning a grand occasion at Barbour Hall for Christmas. You must join us then, mustn't he, Emma?"

Emma could only nod. This was the first she'd heard of any such plans. When Jonathan Ramsey's attention was diverted by yet another admirer, Emma hissed at Lily, "Why did you tell him that? He's terribly forward and rude."

"Nonsense!" laughed Lily. "He has zest for life. These times are too exciting to be slow and boring." Cocking her head to one side, she surveyed Emma, whose fingers were working nervously with the neck of her pink cloak. "Just relax. Tonight, let's have fun . . . and, Emma, we must do something about your hair."

Jonathan Ramsey returned to her side with a bow. His apology for the interruption was delivered with such a candid expression on his boyish, clean-shaven cheeks that Emma began to believe she had judged him too harshly. The cut of his dark, frock-tailed coat and the soft material of his slim, tan trousers told her he was a well-to-do gentleman. Although he was not as tall and dashing as Harrison and lacked the captain's quietly mysterious depths, Jonathan was quite the most fun of anyone she had ever been around. His warmth soon had her giggling like a schoolgirl.

They strolled down Broad Street, a boulevard with a wide median planted with towering magnolias and oaks. Greek Revival and Italianate mansions, each with its own distinctive architecture, graced both sides of the street. While most planters in southeastern Alabama and southwestern Georgia built their houses on their plantations, the planters and merchants of Eufaula built side by side along the town's boulevards. For the past twenty years, thousands of bales of cotton had been shipped down the Chattahoochee to Apalachicola, Florida, the largest cotton-exporting port in America. This exceptional prosperity lent a fairyland opulence which tonight twinkled as though thousands of fireflies fluttered to keep every house ablaze with light. White-coated but-lers bowed the laughing couples through double doors of one house after another.

Each hostess seemed intent upon outdoing the other. Light suppers of oyster patties, lobster, chicken salad, cakes, jellies, ices, shrimps, meringues, tongue, and small hams were arranged in elaborate beauty on gleaming mahogany sideboards ashine with silver.

"I can't eat another morsel," laughed Emma, "— after this." She reached for one more Spanish wind cake. She bit into the meringue which had been slowly baked to a delicate crispness. "Umm," she murmured, savoring the whipped cream filling. Lastly, she popped the pink meringue rosebud into her upturned mouth.

"It's as hard as stealing cream from a cat to get a smile out of you," grinned Ramsey, "but it's surely worth the wait."

"Let's go to the Treadwell house for dancing," interrupted Lily.

As the merry foursome made their way through the torchlit garden, they were stopped by Henry Clayton.

"May I speak with you gentlemen for a moment? Beg pardon, ladies." He bent low with a sweeping gesture.

As the men stepped aside under the sheltering shadow of a glossy-leafed magnolia tree, Emma turned to Lily. "Why did you tell — him?" She swallowed, too insecure to speak Jonathan's name aloud just yet. "Why did you say we were having a big celebration? You know your mother is not feeling well and wants us to have another quiet Christmas in mourning."

"One Christmas in mourning is quite enough," Lily answered firmly. "Papa would want us to celebrate for his grandchild." Suddenly drooping, she pressed her fist against her mouth and whispered, "Oh, I wish he could've seen my pretty one."

Sympathetic at the tears shining in Lily's wide, dark eyes, Emma sighed. She had known neither peace nor joy since her brother, Clare Edwards, had died. She existed alone with Cordelia and Cordelia's adolescent son, Foy, in Barbour Hall.

"I'll come home first thing in the morning and help get started with the work." Lily's voice drew her back.

"You know it isn't the work I'm worried about." An unaccustomed frown creased Emma's forehead. She pulled her quilted moiré wrap more tightly around her slender shoulders and clutched it to her chest with both hands. "I don't know how we'll get ready in four days — I'll manage somehow." She looked down at Lily. "But it's your mama. Most of the time she has me keep the keys, but I can't really do anything without her telling me."

"I'll manage Mama." Lily's voice lacked confidence as she leaned over to incline her ear toward the magnolia tree.

Clayton was speaking urgently. "Gentlemen, we all certainly hope that we can become a sovereign nation which can export its own goods without interference. We pray this will not come to war. If, indeed, it does, we have no army."

"Except the local militia groups," interjected Ramsey.

"But worse," continued Clayton, "we have no navy!"

"A navy will be vital," nodded Harrison. "We have no hope if we cannot navigate our rivers and keep our seaports open. We must have a navy!"

"Then we can count on you gentlemen?" Clayton lowered his voice and stepped further under the tree.

"A navy," gasped Lily, her face paling in the torchlight. "I had not thought — surely Harrison would never have to go to war . . ."

"Come on, ladies," Jonathan Ramsey called gaily. "Hurry. The orchestra's playing the 'Tallahassee Waltz.' "

Drifting through open French doors, the

lilting popular music soothed Emma's frown. Bass notes set their feet sliding to three-quarter time, but the treble trilled up the scale as daintily as a minuet. Unaccustomed to dancing, Emma feared her feet would be as wooden and useless as Minerva's, but, oh, how she longed to dance! His black brows raised quizzically, Mr. Ramsey bowed before her with an exaggerated wave of his arm. Lifting her clear, sweet face to his, she stood motionless for a moment, hands raised, lips parted, eyes wide. Slowly, she stretched out her hand and let him lead her to the dance floor. He seemed not to notice the questions in her innocent blue eyes or the fears pulsating the veins beneath her crystal necklace.

Sweeping her along in the confident curve of his arm, he guided her forward to the right, forward to the left, then sliding backwards. Laughing, she stumbled through the reverse steps.

"Relax." He chuckled good-humoredly. "Just float where I — and the music — take you."

Whirling, swaying, her hoop tilting her pink velvet skirt to the rhythm of the music and making the iridescent beading shimmer, Emma began to feel as happy as a schoolgirl, as giddy as a child on a swing.

After several dances, Jonathan brought two punch cups and ushered her to the coolness of the garden. Walking silently through the sharp-scented borders of black-green boxwood, they settled on a marble bench invitingly placed before a blossom-laden camellia bush.

Her breath coming in quick gasps, her cheeks flushed, Emma said, "I don't know when I've had such fun!" Golden tendrils were escaping around her damp forehead, and she tried in vain to secure them.

"Miss Emma, how lovely you are," Jonathan said softly. "You are as delicate and perfect as these camellias." He plucked a waxy pink blossom and gently presented it to her, gazing at her for a long moment. Then he said seriously, "You didn't seem to second Miss Lily's invitation for Christmas. Dare I hope that you might welcome me?"

"Oh, of course, of course," Emma responded quickly with her eyes sparkling. "We couldn't have you spend such a special day in a hotel, Mr. Ramsey. Besides, it wouldn't seem a party without you." She dropped her lashes, and her cheeks flushed pinker for letting this slip out.

If she had thought him forward, what would he think of her?

Jonathan Ramsey laughed heartily. "Then,

of course, I'll be there."

Emma's glow remained as they returned to the dancing.

When at last the evening had to end and they left her at Barbour Hall, her euphoria continued. Putting on her flannelette nightgown, she hugged herself and laughed softly, as full of anticipation as a child about to hang up her first stocking. She climbed the needlepoint-covered stool onto the high, rosewood bed, laid the camellia on the pillow beside her cheek, and snuggled into the feather mattress. With her mind flitting, whirling, dancing, she lay staring happily at the airy white mesh which covered the lilting curve of the rosewood canopy.

A sudden gust of wind lengthened the shadow of her candle. The loose knots of the diamond-patterned macramé canopy became a giant spider web against the ceiling.

Quickly blowing out the candle, she closed her eyes, exhausted. Just as she dozed into a pleasant dream, a rasping voice snatched her back.

"Emma! Em-mah!"

CHAPTER 3

"Emmaaa . . . ," Cordelia Edwards whined.

Sighing, Emma climbed down from the bed, threw a blue flannel wrapper over her gown, and padded across the drafty hall to her sister-in-law's large, square room at the rear of the second floor.

Enthroned upon a massive bed with straight, walnut bedposts holding aloft a walnut canopy, Cordelia Edwards parted the wine velvet bed curtains and peered out as Emma set her candle on the marble-top bedside table. Her face pursed into a pout, she said, "I didn't think you'd leave me for so long. You stayed out half the night. My rheumatism is paining miserably." She sank weakly against the goose-down pillows. "You'd best make me a mustard plaster."

Emma complied as quickly as possible, making apologies, even though she knew that Mrs. Edwards's personal maid, Kitty, could have mixed the hot water, dry mustard, and flour as well as she.

Spreading the sour-smelling paste on a clean cloth and folding it carefully to keep it from oozing, she applied the poultice to Cordelia's broad back. She refilled the copper kettle at the Wedgwood lavatory in the dressing room and replaced it on the hearth. She sighed, thankful that her brother had been far ahead of his time and installed a cistern in the attic which was filled by a windmill for a ready supply of gravity-forced, running water. She sat shivering by the banked coals until the poultice had sufficiently reddened Cordelia's soft flesh and she could remove it. Dawn was streaking the sky as she climbed wearily into bed.

When Emma awoke, it was with a slow luxurious stretching and a smiling remembrance of her pleasant evening. Suddenly she sat bolt upright. Sunlight streamed through her eastern window, danced around the blue walls, and hopscotched over the blue and white Oriental rug. How had she slept so long? Cordelia Edwards's voice rumbled from the morning room.

Jumping down from the bed, Emma ran to her dressing room, grasped the German silver faucets of the lavatory, and splashed cool water on her face. Hurrying into a faded calico, she hesitated to open her door into the small sitting room which adjoined. Instead, she stepped to the wide, central hall and peeped through the sliding doors that closed off one end to form the morning room. She stood stiffly, trying to determine her sister-in-law's mood and adjust herself before she entered.

Laughter surprised her. There sat Lily bubbling with good spirits and actually eating eggs and greasy sausage. Emma slipped quietly into the cozy room and queasily took only coffee from the laden breakfast tray. Lily, feeding Mignonne, who sat beside her on the small sofa, had already convinced her mother that what she needed to make her feel good again was a joyous Christmas celebration. Cordelia relaxed against the comfortable upholstery of the gracefully curving Louis XV style furniture and rapidly formulated menus.

"Foy and I will be in charge of decorating." Lily smiled fondly at her fourteen-year-old brother, who sat with his long legs dangling over the window seat.

"You bet," he croaked excitedly. His childhood chubbiness had melted into hollows and angles. Although he tried to move with dignity befitting his advancing years, his natural exuberance overcame him. He hopped down and started for the door with his dark eyes sparkling. "I'll find a perfect tree — and I know where some mistletoe —"

"You be careful climbing treetops after mistletoe," warned his mother, as she finished her buttered biscuits and fig preserves. "Take Lige with you."

"Yes, Ma'am." Foy grinned, leaving the room with his long arms and legs flapping like an excited scarecrow.

Emma sat at the small French secretary of light beechwood and made lists at Cordelia's direction. The fluttering in her stomach calmed and her anticipation grew. When Lily rose to leave, her words brought a blush to Emma's smooth face.

"I must go home and dispatch Harrison and Jonathan on a turkey hunt."

"Emma and I will start cooking," answered her mother. Paying no attention to Emma's pink cheeks and downcast eyelashes, Cordelia led the way downstairs and across the suspended, covered walkway to the separate brick kitchen.

The cook, Aunt Dilsey, scowled when Mrs. Edwards shunted her aside to make her own special cake. Aunt Dilsey soon recovered her authority, and her broad face beamed beneath her red bandanna as she put the young girls to various tasks of seed-ing raisins, cutting orange peel, and chopping the candied citron. Disdainfully setting aside the pecans, which could be picked up in the yard and eaten anytime, she directed two girls in cracking and picking out the almonds, English walnuts, and the Christmas favorite, Brazil nuts, which had come up the Chattahoochee on the steamboats returning for more bales of cotton. With everyone working, Dilsey herself began cooking sweet potatoes in a huge iron pot hanging on an arm over the open fire. Soon she had turned them into a custard which filled the small building with the fragrance of cinnamon.

"No hog-killin', no Chris'mus, seems to me," pouted old Patience.

"Too hot for that. We'll have to make do with cured ham from the smokehouse," laughed Emma, pushing wet curls from her forehead with a sticky forearm. She and dark, long-boned Kitty worked together over a wide, earthen bowl. Orange juice dripped over their hands into the bowl as they cut sections, carefully removing seeds and membrane, and mixed in coconut. Sprinkling on sugar, Emma stirred and tasted the ambrosia. "Perfect." She smiled at Kitty with a self-satisfied glow, glad that she had purchased the oranges and coconut when the last steamboat came up from the seaport of Apalachicola. Celebration or not, it would not be Christmas without ambrosia.

Aunt Dilsey had evidently felt that way about fruitcake. Gleefully, she produced a covered box and let them all have a sniff of the dark, rich cakes she had made weeks ago and set to ripen.

Red-faced from the warmth of the kitchen, Mrs. Edwards laughed and joked with her servants as she placed her cake, made delicate with stiffly beaten egg whites, in the oven built into the brick wall by the fireplace. She did not yet trust the new iron cookstove in the corner for baking.

When Cordelia and Emma left the kitchen at last and walked back across the high, covered walkway to the house, they heard Dilsey's mellow voice pouring forth in song:

"There's a star in the east on Christmas
    morn.
    Rise up, shepherd, and fol-ler;
It'll lead to the place where the Savior's
    born,
    Rise up, shepherd, and fol-ler."
The younger servants answered in rich
    harmony:

"Fol-ler, Fol-ler, rise up, shepherd, and
   fol-ler,
Fol-ler de star of Beth-le-hem,
   Rise up, shepherd, and fol-ler."

They stood for a moment on the porch to
cool and catch their breath and to listen as
one group chanted a line and another
echoed back the refrain.

"Leave yo' sheep and leave yo' lambs,
   Rise up, shepherd, and fol-ler.
Leave yo' ewes and leave yo' rams,
   Rise up, shepherd, and fol-ler.
Take good heed to de an-gel's word,
   Rise up, shepherd, and fol-ler,
You'll forget your sheep, you'll forget your
   herd,
   Rise up, shepherd, and fol-ler."

As they stepped into the house, the sharp
fragrance of freshly cut pine filled the wide
central hallway. Cordelia flopped on the sofa
of shiny, slick, black horsehair. It was her
favorite piece of furniture because the style
of its unusual S–shaped legs dated to 1783
and had been made for only a period of ten
years. Declaring herself too tired to move
farther than this spot at the rear of the hall,
she leaned back and surveyed her children's
handiwork. Lily had returned, and she and

Foy had made ropes of black-green pine, which they hung in swags from the chair rail down both sides of the long hall.

"Come look!" Lily pulled a weary Emma across the black-and-white marble floor, threw open the double entrance doors, and pushed her onto the veranda. Pine garlands also hung in each interval between the pairs of white columns.

Grinning from ear to ear, Lige carried in a stepladder. Foy followed, carefully holding a branch of waxy, delicate green leaves with tiny white berries. With great ceremony he climbed the ladder and fastened the mistletoe to the crown-of-thorns chandelier, a unique ring of six-pointed stars, stabbed with crystal thorns and hung with varying crystal teardrops.

"It was so high in the treetops that I had to shoot it down," Foy said proudly as he jumped from the ladder and looked up at his prize. "That gives me the honor of claiming the first kiss." With a bony arm he swiftly pulled Lily beneath the mistletoe. His ears stood out beet red from his bristly hair as he planted a shy kiss on her cheek.

For the next two days, the house rang with laughter, singing, scurrying footsteps, and rattling paper. Foy joined Harrison and Jonathan in the hunt, and they came in with quail and dove to supplement the turkey and ham. With each trip from the woods, Foy brought more holly until every spot, even the picture frames, glowed with green leaves and scarlet berries. Cordelia Edwards had taken back the huge ring of keys which denoted authority over the house, but only when Emma was very tired did the old feeling of not belonging overshadow her happiness. She tried to remind herself that Mr. Ramsey was a stranger passing through, and she should not let her heart beat faster at the thought of him; but the sound of Jonathan's laughter, even if from another room, always brought a peaceful smile to her face.

Food baskets were packed for the poor. "All my dear Mr. Edwards's good works must be continued, of course," his widow declared with a catch in her voice and tears shining in her eyes.

Each evening after supper, they settled contentedly in the parlor around the fire. Mrs. Edwards was careful to shield herself from the heat by using the face screen, ornamented with a picture of English ladies and gentlemen, worked in gold, silver, and china beads. She could not allow the paraffin she used to conceal wrinkles to melt. They took turns reading passages from

Charles Dickens's *Christmas Carol.* When Emma's time came to sit by the fine Argand lamp and read by the sperm oil flame, she was extremely conscious of Jonathan's warm eyes upon her.

Lily and Foy strictly forbade anyone's entering the music room until Christmas Eve. When Lily arrived at first dark with Harrison behind her quietly carrying Mignonne, she signaled Foy and called to her mother, "Come on, Mama, it's time. Now, you're going to hang up your stocking, too!"

Ceremoniously, she slid open the doors of red Bohemian etched glass and revealed a tremendous cedar tree standing in the center of the room, with myriads of candles twinkling from its branches.

"Look, Baby, see the pretty tree."

Mignonne gazed at the flickering lights in wonder and stretched out dimpled hands. Harrison held her close to see the various ornaments — a spun-glass swan, a dog carrying a golden basket in his mouth, a bunch of green grapes imported from Germany when Lily was an infant, and other crystal or tinseled treasures. Then he handed her to his wife and stationed himself in the corner near the buckets of water, just in case of fire.

Oblivious to the fact that she was gowned

40

in sumptuous emerald velvet especially ordered for her from the Paris Salon of Charles Frederick Worth, Lily sat on the floor beside the tree. Candlelight glistened on her creamy bare shoulders and the magnificent diamond and emerald necklace which had belonged to Harrison's French grandmother. Rivaling the tree for sparkle, Lily showed Mignonne the Christmas garden. Set amid cotton snow were miniature houses, shepherds, and sheep. Lily lifted the tiny manger and told her infant daughter about the baby Jesus. Harrison read aloud the second chapter of Luke.

"Now it's time to 'hang the stockings by the chimney with care,' " quoted Foy.

"Why, where is yours, Emma?" Lily demanded of the girl standing in the shadows. "Go to your room and get one this minute!"

After Emma had complied obediently, she was directed to the square piano which had been pushed awry so that the tree would be reflected in the towering pier mirror between the floor-to-ceiling windows. Carefully she lifted her skirt of shimmering, ice-blue taffeta around the piano stool. Her fingers moved lovingly over the mother-of-pearl keys of the beautifully carved rosewood instrument. When she was playing beautiful music and lifting her clear soprano in song, she came nearest to grasping Lily's belief that God smiled with love upon each individual.

A stirring in the hallway interrupted "Hark! The Herald Angels Sing." Jonathan Ramsey had arrived. Voicing jovial greetings and filling the room with laughter, he smiled appreciatively at Emma's gown, which was trimmed with a fichu of creamy lace. She had no sparkling jewels, only a cameo nestled in the lace and opal earrings; but she had tied a blue velvet ribbon midway on her slender neck. Taking Lily's advice, she had loosened her honey-colored hair from its usual severe knot into soft masses of ringlets.

Emma had spent a great deal of time on her toilette; now, however, she nervously clutched her cameo. She should not have presumed to dress for a dance until she secured permission to go. Her blue eyes darted toward her sister-in-law who was wearing her most put-upon expression.

"Uh," Emma cleared her throat, "don't you think I'd better stay with you and Mignonne — and Foy? All of the servants have left for the setting up at their church — you know, to watch for the coming of Christ as they always do on Christmas Eve . . ."

"Has everyone gone?" Cordelia queried

brusquely.

"Yes, Ma'am," Emma replied meekly. "Even feeble old Patience said she must not let her Lord catch her in bed on the night when the very cows fall on their knees."

"Don't you think you can manage, Mama?" interjected Lily. "Everyone who is anyone is going to the party in John Clark's new building."

"I'll play with Mignonne 'til she gets sleepy," volunteered Foy with a crooked, loving smile toward his aunt.

It was agreed upon, and Emma went for her wrap. When she descended the stairs with a rustle of crinoline and a drifting scent of lavender, Jonathan was paying no attention to her. He and Foy were engaged in a grinning, motioning byplay. As she stepped down onto the marble floor, Foy edged her beneath the crown-of-thorns chandelier, and Jonathan reached a swift arm about her slender waist and brushed the merest whisper of a kiss across her lips.

Stiffening in surprise, she gasped and stared with wide blue eyes. He grinned and silently pointed to the mistletoe. Cordelia's face puffed in shock, but for the rest of the evening, Emma tingled with a notion of floating two inches above the dance floor.

■ ■ ■ ■

Mysterious rustlings awakened Emma. A smile twitched about her lips, but she pretended she was asleep and kept her eyes squeezed shut.

"Chris'mus gif'!" shouted a voice as her bedroom door was thrust open. "I s'prise you!"

"Oh, you caught me," laughed Emma, sitting up in the bed. She handed over silver coins from a pouch beside the bed.

Kitty chuckled and Tildy squealed in delight. Emboldened, they crossed the hall to Cordelia Edwards's room and burst in, repeating the cry, "Chris'mus gif'!"

Smiling that the day was properly begun, Emma went to the window and parted the lace curtains. The sun was well up, but the air was crisp and cold. *Good,* she thought, *this is more like Christmas.* It would also be more comfortable for the last-minute cooking, she knew. Humming as she dressed, Emma secured the leather pouch to her belt in preparation for further surprises.

The pungent aroma of coffee drew her along that walkway to the kitchen. Aunt Dilsey had already fried the salty, cured ham and was pouring coffee in the grease to make the red-eye gravy. Biscuits, baked in the Dutch oven surrounded by hot coals on the hearth, waited, crusty brown on the outside, fluffy on the inside. A large platter was heaped with oysters.

"Wait to cook the eggs until Lily arrives — oh, I hear them now!" Emma hurried out to get a hug and kiss from Mignonne before Cordelia claimed her.

After breakfast, Foy lighted the candles on the Christmas tree and importantly distributed the stockings and gifts. Delighted exclamations and thanks followed each opening of books, lace collars and cuffs, silver dishes, and so on. Then the happy group trouped out to see Lily's present from Harrison, a pretty carriage with a perfectly matched pair of ponies. Emma turned toward the kitchen.

" 'Martha, Martha, don't be cumbered about much serving,' " quoted Lily, frowning when she saw that Emma was not going to church with the rest of the family. "Really, Emma, you must also feed the soul! Worship and fellowship can refresh and strengthen you for your tasks. . . ."

Emma shrugged Lily's hand off of her shoulder and stood firm. She wished that Lily would not press her. Attending church was simply one more obligation in her duty-

45

filled life. Cordelia did not care whether she was included; certainly God could not care about her insignificant life.

After completing dinner preparations, she went upstairs to change into a pale pink wool frock. Wide navy ribbon banded the two-yard hem and rose at intervals halfway up the skirt in a club design. This was repeated on the matching knee-length jacket which she laid carefully over the bed. Returning downstairs, she heard a commotion on the front porch.

"Chris'mus gif'. I seed you first!"

She watched through the sidelights of the door as Jonathan delivered a coin to a small boy with mock surprise and protestation. "That's not fair. You only caught me because you slipped up barefooted as a yard dog." He laughed.

Emma opened the doors, laughing, and Jonathan made her an elaborate bow.

"Please, don't think me forward," he said quite seriously. "I know we've just met, but do accept a small token of my esteem." He held out a nosegay of violets and geraniums.

Accepting the bouquet with a flush of pleasure, Emma ushered him into the parlor where they chatted until the family burst in.

A glow of happiness radiated from Emma's face as it had not in the years since she had earned the title "spinster". The snowy damask gleamed, the polished silver sparkled, the best Spode china basked beneath perfect food. The turkey was delicately browned; the doves, delightfully crisp; the vegetables, perfectly seasoned — each in turn drew exclamations of "Best I ever tasted."

The meal was eaten slowly with a great deal of happy talk. At last, they moved to the parlor and languished by the fire, half-dozing while enjoying comfortable silences and idle chatter.

Popping firecrackers roused them at last. While Lily bundled the baby, Emma ran to her room where she donned her pink coat and added a hat made of navy ribbon. Burying her face in the nosegay, she sighed with the happiness of blossoming love. Carefully pressing a geranium leaf and a violet between the pages of her new book, she plucked three more violets and pinned them to the neck of her jacket.

When they rejoined the men, Harrison wore a Spanish costume with red trousers and a tremendous hat while Jonathan sported a clown costume of yellow. With his mouth pursed in mock seriousness and his eyes popping, he tipped a hat as small as a teacup and escorted Emma to the wagon.

Foy, in the funniest costume he could improvise, peered with snapping eyes through his doughface, a papier-mâché mask. He had decorated the wagon and even put crepe paper on the mules. He handed out drums and bugles, and they piled aboard and drove into the street to join other wagons and outlandishly costumed, masked riders on horseback in the annual celebration known as the Fantastic Rides. The noisy merrymakers moved about the streets in an impromptu parade, then headed north toward Roseland, the plantation owned by Colonel Toney and his wife, who were renowned for elaborate entertainments. Long before they reached the house, guns answered with joyful blasts their noisy announcement in lieu of church bells that "Christ is born!"

After refreshments with the Toneys, the group returned more quietly into town. Shadows were lengthening, and Emma shivered with a sudden chill as they met first the Pioneer Guards and then Brannon's Zouaves out marching in full force. Oblivious to the usual Christmas merrymakers, the militia groups drilled seriously.

"We'd better get out of these costumes," said Harrison under his breath to Jonathan. "Captain Baker is entertaining the Eufaula

Rifles and we're expected."

Lily's dark eyes were wide and liquid as she clutched Emma's flowing sleeve.

"Yes," agreed Jonathan, "they will want you there. With your knowledge of the Chattahoochee and the depths of Apalachicola Bay, you will play an important part in defense —"

Harrison frowned and shook his head.

As they entered at the rear of the hall, the happiness of the day seemed to be cracking and breaking into jagged pieces like a broken mirror.

Harrison lifted Mignonne high into the air to make her laugh before he kissed her good-bye.

As the men started down the steps, Jonathan's voice drifted behind his departing back. "This might be the last Christmas as we know it for a very long time. Seeing you with Mignonne makes me realize, too late, that I should have spent it with my daughter."

CHAPTER 4

His daughter! Aghast, Emma flung one clutching hand to her chest and with the other stifled the thought that threatened to become a scream. Paralyzed for a moment, she wrenched her feet from the floor and ran across the back hall. No one saw her as she escaped up the hidden staircase.

Slamming through the door to her bedroom, she snatched the violets and geraniums from their vase and threw them across the floor. "How could you? How could you?" she whimpered through clenched teeth. She stamped around the room with her kidskin slippers grinding each blossom and leaf into the blue and white rug. From below, Mignonne's cries bellowed forth, alerting everyone, punishing everyone who did not immediately rush to her aid. Gulping tears, Emma wished she could make someone attend to her hurting. Shivering like a puppy which had been patted on the head and then kicked, she stood in the center of the huge room, small and forlorn.

Reprimanding herself, she fought for control. Her tears congealed. Looking down at her feet, she winced. Angry purple and red and green smears stained the valuable Oriental rug. Sighing, she realized that the nosegay had meant nothing to such a worldly man. She had judged him a roué from the beginning; why had she not remembered? Dry-eyed, she jerked back her head and flung her arms, cross-wristed, upon it. The kiss — merely a prank under the mistletoe.

A rattle at the window caused her to part the lace curtains and peer through the wavery glass. The shiny carriage with its prancing ponies was moving away.

"Oh, Lily, how could you?" she whispered in anguish as she leaned her forehead against the cold windowpane.

Lily had said, "Have fun, just for tonight." She, of course, did not know that Emma's twenty-seven-year-old spinster's heart beat as foolishly as any schoolgirl's.

Suddenly bone-cold and weak with exhaustion, Emma crawled beneath the quilts, coat and all. Piling pillows over her head, she sobbed as she had not allowed herself to do since she was sixteen.

Emma was glad that Lily did not visit during the next two days. She imagined herself lashing out at her with angry words; however, when she heard Lily's lilting voice floating up the staircase, she knew that she did not want to face her niece and tried to escape her by running down the hidden back stairs which the servants used. But Lily saw her.

"Oh, Emma, there you are. Fort Moultrie has been burned — why, whatever is wrong with you?" She stared in surprise at Emma's face which was pinched and blue.

"N–nothing," replied Emma. "Nothing's wrong," she said in a weak whine. Her shoulders slumped dejectedly.

"Something is wrong!" Lily stamped her foot. "Are you ill? What's the matter?"

"Why didn't you tell me?"

"Tell you what?"

"That he — Jonathan's — married."

Lily's dark eyes filled with sudden understanding and sympathy. Taking Emma's hand, she pulled her into the blue and white bedroom and led her to the wing chair by the fireplace. Looking down at the older girl, she said solemnly, "He's not married."

Emma, huddling miserably between the sheltering wings of the chair, watched Lily throw kindling on the fire and poke it into a blaze before she spoke. "Yes, he is," she said sadly. "I heard him mention his daughter."

"No, he isn't," Lily said firmly. She drew the carved cherry rocker close and chafed Emma's cold hands. "He was. His wife died in childbirth. Two years ago. He owns a tremendous cotton plantation over near Savannah. But he hasn't stayed there much since she died —" She bowed her shining, dark hair and said softly, "Oh, Emma, I'm sorry. I didn't think to tell you."

"It's all right." Emma's voice rang hollowly in her ears as she fought for composure.

"No, no, it's not. You've been miserable, and it's all my fault. I didn't stop to think — I only meant for you to enjoy the parties — the holidays . . ."

The fire crackled merrily. Color returned to Emma's cheeks as relief flowed through her. Now it was Lily who drooped dejectedly.

"It's all right," Emma repeated, patting her lovingly.

"I'm not too sure." The younger girl threw back her curls and looked into her aunt's eyes with worry. "Are you falling so much in love?"

"Yes." Emma laughed shakily. "But if he's not married, what's wrong with that?"

"Well, he's always here, there, or the other place. Since Betty died he's been rambling the world. I'm not sure he's over her. All his joking might be to mask his emptiness. And besides that — with all this war talk, men are too occupied to have time to think of love," she finished in a rush.

Emma sat silently, trying to still her fluttering hands. The muscles of her pale face twitched as she struggled to erase the pain.

"Everything about the secession has seemed so exciting," Lily reflected slowly, "but since I've heard about Fort Moultrie's being burned, I've begun to feel that a huge black net is hanging over us, just waiting to drop."

Relieved to change the topic from her own problems, Emma coughed and brought her voice to its normal melodious register. "I've had a strange, uneasy feeling ever since last October when we were in Montgomery, while Douglas was campaigning for the presidency. Do you remember the torchlight procession when Douglas was egged? I can still see that short, square figure with eggs breaking against it."

Lily laughed shortly and chattered on. "Yes, but the picture that comes back to me is of Janie's wedding party when a man rushed in saying, 'Lincoln is elected.' The words fell like a pall. You could see the Southern spirit as it leaped into the eyes of the men. It seemed thrilling then to have our honor defended, but I was really frightened that night with all the men out, armed and equipped, expecting trouble." Lily paused and searched Emma's vulnerable face with a frown.

When she resumed speaking, her words came slowly, deliberately. "Then the threat of riot seemed to blow over, and everyone began to say we could declare our sovereignty and independence; it became exciting — but, oh, Emma," she wailed, "this is not the time to fall in love!"

Icy drizzle chilled New Year's Eve. News was received of the resignation of the President's cabinet at Washington City. At dawn on the first day of 1861, the temperature plummeted to twenty degrees. The unaccustomed ice killed the flowers.

Cordelia took to her bed against the damp cold. Waiting upon her, Emma was closely confined. Each day she stood peering out her lace curtains, her heart beating with the drums which assembled the Eufaula Rifles and Pioneer Guards for drilling. She tried not to focus on the unaccustomed sight of jagged icicles dripping from the eaves. They seemed too much to mirror the painful, useless thawing within her breast.

" 'Not the time to fall in love,' " she whispered against the cold, wavery glass. "He hasn't given me another thought."

The temperature crept back up above the freezing mark, but then cold, gray rain fell for several days without letup. Shivering, unable to get warm in the high-ceilinged house which was designed for the three seasons of hot, humid weather, the family speculated on the disasters which would result if the temperature again dropped to freezing.

At last, on the tenth of January, the sun shone brilliantly and the blue sky sparkled. Emma was setting the big pots of ferns back on the front porch when she glimpsed a figure rounding the red cedars at the gate. Pressing her hand to her heart as if she could still its beating, she tried to force herself to be calm. She turned slowly and said as coolly as possible, "Good morning, Mr. Ramsey."

"Good morning," he called cheerily, bounding up the steps to the high porch. "You're as blue and gold and lovely as the day." He smiled, taking her hand.

Lowering her eyelashes shyly, she looked down at her faded gray dress and knew he was complimenting her eyes and hair. A small, pleased smile touched her lips.

"Everything is coming to a head," Jonathan said seriously, plunging into conversation with no apology for his failure to thank her for Christmas dinner. "Have you heard the news today?"

Solemnly she shook her golden curls. She could not tell him that all her thoughts had centered on him. The way he moved, with rapid, jerking gestures, and talked, in quick bursts, told Emma he had been far too busy to think of her.

"Mississippi passed her Ordinance of Secession yesterday! They made provisions for a state army and appointed the Honorable Jefferson Davis her major general." His eyes flashed with excitement. "They seized the fort on Ship Island and the U.S. Hospital on the Mississippi River — and at any moment a telegram should come saying Florida has seceded."

"What of Alabama?"

"The state convention is in secret session. The vote will be taken tomorrow." He paused, his eyes gentle upon her face, as he said softly, "Will you do me the honor of accompanying me to the celebrations when it is announced?"

"You're sure, then, of the outcome?"

"Of course!"

Emma snapped a dead frond from the fern and crumpled it in her hand. He had mentioned the river installations, but her questions about his part in all this lodged in her throat.

Jonathan stood waiting. His dark curls bobbed as he earnestly asked again, "You'll come with me?"

"I don't know — I — you know Cordelia . . ." Her face was clouded with uncertainty.

"But the main party is to be given by Lewis Llewellen Cato. Surely she will want to go to her neighbor's house."

"I don't know. I just — can't — say. We'll see."

"I'll be here to get you," he said confidently. Squeezing her hand as he bent swiftly over it in a perfunctory bow, he hurried away. He turned at the gate and waved. " 'Til tomorrow," he called.

She sat on the steps in the pale sunshine with her chin in her hands. What should she do? It was clearly evident that Lily was right. He had merely been seeking diversion for the holidays. His only interest lay in the silly politics. She could protect herself if she used her sister-in-law as an excuse and stayed safely in Barbour Hall. She wanted to be near him, to absorb his vitality, to laugh at his funny stories, to feel the warmth of his twinkling eyes, to touch — she choked on the surging emotion and dropped her head to her knees. Numbness hurt less.

Jerking her chin up, she gritted her teeth. She would not let him make her cry. She simply would not go. When Alabama's fate was decided, he would leave Eufaula and she would never have to see him again.

"Em-ma," Cordelia's voice summoned, unsettling her completely.

On January 11, the sun blessed the day with warmth. Everyone moved about quietly, expectantly. Waiting. Suddenly at two in the afternoon, church bells began to toll. Rejoicing, the people filled the street, shouting, "Great news! Alabama has left the Union that would make slaves of us!" Spreading the lace curtains at the window where she stood, Emma was struck with the sobering thought that their state was now sovereign and independent.

"The old bonds are broken." Cordelia voiced her thoughts as she thrust her head in at the bedroom door. "Come, it's time we were going to the Catos'."

Emma lifted troubled eyes to her sister-in-law's face. As usual, her plans were decided for her. "I'll hurry and change," she replied soberly, but she remained immobile, staring out of the window. "I know they are defending what they believe to be their rights, but many of them are so young." She sighed and pointed down to the group called Brannon's Zouaves, mere boys parading in Turkish-style costumes.

"Much of the best blood of our boys will be spilt, I fear," said Cordelia, peering out. "I can't help being glad that Foy is too young to volunteer."

As they stood bound in spirit for a moment, Foy came loping across the lawn with arms and legs flying. He joined a group of boys shooting fireworks. Sighing and shaking their heads, the women turned and began to prepare for the party.

Half-sorry, half-glad that she could not wait for Jonathan Ramsey, Emma accompanied Cordelia down the street. Just as they reached the Catos' hitching post, the cannon blasted. Emma steadied herself by hanging onto the iron horsehead. She twisted her nose at the acrid smell as the cannon fired one hundred rounds in honor of the occasion. Halfway through, she could bear it no longer and clapped her hands over her ears. At last the nerve-racking blasts ended, and she opened her eyes.

Jonathan stood beside her, laughing. Taking her by the elbow of her pink wool coat, he guided her down the central walk to the house. On each side, angled pathways invited strolls through boxwood-edged diamonds and triangles of formal, symmetrical flower beds. Her steps lagged as she looked toward a display of spring bulbs.

"Hurry," he said. "Colonel Cato is about to introduce Yancey." His springing step bespoke his excitement as he pushed her to a spot in front of the white clapboard Greek Revival mansion.

William Lowndes Yancey came through the double entrance doors and stood on the wide porch, majestically set off with thirteen square, white columns across the front and around the sides of the house. With a great show of oratory, he expounded the Southern Rights' position.

Standing amid the cheering crowd, Emma had never felt so alone. She wondered why Jonathan had asked her to join him. He had given her such flattering attention during the Christmas festivities; now, he scarcely noticed her presence. Throwing back her head, she looked up at the large, pillared observatory set high atop the steep roof. This cupola was an exact replica of the first story.

I'm like that, she thought. *A fake. A shell*

with no life stirring within me.

Clapping vigorously, Jonathan led a cheer. When the din had subsided, he smiled down at Emma with his eyes gleaming and said enthusiastically, "The South can never be conquered!"

White-coated servants began moving among the guests with huge trays of refreshments. Jonathan declared, "I'm famished," and led Emma to a laden table set beneath a huge oak. Demurely she accepted a tall, slender goblet of syllabub, a fashionable dessert made by churning milk, cream, and cider, and nibbled a petit four. Watching Jonathan pile a plate with dainty party food, Emma wondered why she had ever thought him less handsome than Harrison. His face was always set in such a sweet expression; his dark eyes always twinkled. And that curl of dark hair tumbling over his forehead — She sighed, breathed the sweet fragrance of the narcissus which had recovered from the cold and bloomed again, and longed to reach up and smooth the curl back in place.

"You're mighty quiet today." He smiled down at her.

"Yes," she replied shakily. "It's all so — so overwhelming. I — I — just . . ." she stammered. Afraid that he would see the longing in her eyes, she dropped her eyelashes and concentrated on tracing the blocks of navy ribbon on her pink skirt.

"Yes, everything is moving swiftly now," he said briskly. "I'll wager Georgia will leave the Union by next week."

"Oh?"

Jonathan paused with a pecan tasse midway to his mouth and considered the small, hurt sound.

"I guess that means you'll be going home?" She lifted her eyes to memorize his face.

Delighted, he popped the bite-size pie into his mouth, crunched, and laughed. "Then I take it you'd miss me?"

"Why should I?" She turned away, angry with herself that she had betrayed her emotions. "I've hardly seen you enough to miss you." She started down a path between tall nandina bushes laden with large clusters of red berries.

"Wait!" He caught her shoulders and turned her toward him. "I'm sorry I laughed. I wasn't laughing at you. I thought perhaps you feel as I . . ."

Her face still clouded, Emma tried to shrug off his grasp.

"To answer your question," he said candidly, still holding her firmly, "I won't be going home. I have to make another quick trip to Montgomery — that's where I've been." He pulled her closer. "I apologize for not coming by since Christmas to thank you. I've been so busy. We're working to form a Confederacy of Southern States . . ." He paused, inhaled, breathed softly, sweetly against the golden ringlets escaping around her forehead. "Lovely Emma. I do care. If we only had more time!"

She ceased her struggle. Gazing into his face as it moved down toward hers, she tried to read his eyes, tried to see if her love was mirrored there.

"Ah, Ramsey, there you are."

Jonathan dropped his hands from her shoulders and turned toward the brusque voice. Her face blazing with shame, she stumbled backward.

"I must speak with you," the man continued. "The revenue cutter, *Lewis Cass* and the tender, *Alert,* belonging to the lighthouse establishment, were seized at Mobile by the state. We must get volunteers together for a navy to man . . ."

Emma wandered away, unnoticed. Their lovely moment had been shattered. Plucking a shriveled brown bud from a camellia bush, she threw it savagely, wishing she had never met Jonathan Ramsey. The promise of winter flowers had been spoiled by the unexpected freeze. Biting her lip and fighting back tears, she pulled the dead buds and wished that she could have remained as she was, moving through life with outward calm, never allowing herself to feel. That was better than being raw, bleeding.

Lily was bouncing toward her, eyes flashing and cheeks rosy from the crisp air. Unable to bear gaiety at the moment, Emma sought to get away.

"Does Cordelia need me?" she asked with a quiver in her voice. She turned toward the house and tried to pull a smooth mask over her face.

"No, no, Mama is sitting by the fire with Miss Martha Jane and the other ladies." Lily's attention was on retying the green satin streamers of her bonnet. "Come join the party. Professor Van Houten is assembling the orchestra in the gazebo." She tugged at Emma's hand, which was cold in spite of the kid gloves. "Relax. Have fun."

Unable to escape, Emma followed her through the grandly formal garden toward the gazebo in back. J. C. Van Houten was tapping his way ahead of them with his gold-headed cane. Just as the blind musician lifted his baton to start the orchestra, Harrison and Jonathan joined them.

For the rest of the party, Jonathan remained at her side, laughing, joking, charming her. Unable to stem the love spilling over the moss-covered dams of her heart, she smiled at him adoringly.

It was only when the celebration ended and evening's chill began to fall that fear and turmoil, churning within, caused her to have difficulty swallowing.

CHAPTER 5

The rousing blast of the steamboat's whistle startled Emma, and the porcelain bowl in her hand crashed to the floor, showering her with fragments. She had thought that she was ready to face this day. Now she knew that she was not. The insistent drone drew her outside. From the porch she could see black puffs of smoke which punctuated shortened blasts. Clutching her fists to her chest, she shivered. The past weeks had flown so swiftly that she had not had time to dread today.

Emma had been swept into the excitement which had gripped Eufaula from the moment of Alabama's secession. Since the Catos' party, men had filled the streets, drilling; women had sat by the fire, sewing. Emma's hands had moved swiftly as her heart pulsed to the rhythm of Jonathan's words, "I do care."

Suddenly alive, a part of the world, she

happily participated in the outfitting of the first troops that marched in uniforms provided by Mary Magdalen Treadwell. Helping to make the banner for the soldiers, Emma had been too busy to dwell on their leaving. Whenever Jonathan and Emma were not working with their respective groups, Jonathan had been constantly at her side. The war preparations and imminent departure accelerated their urgency to talk. They spoke in quick snatches, hopping from one subject to another as they tried to find out minute details about each other's thoughts and lives.

Suddenly, they fell silent. As they attended a party for departing soldiers, Jonathan's humor became forced. Emma's throat constricted, stifling speech. They stood stiffly in a corner with smiles frozen upon their faces. The back of his hand brushed hers. She looked up at him, her eyes filled with love.

The next morning, February 2, 1861, two companies from the county, the Pioneer Guards and the Clayton Guards, left to join the service of the state in the First Alabama Infantry. Emma watched with tears in her eyes as they marched away, proudly bearing the ladies' banners. Dangling on a slender thread of emotion since Jonathan's declaration to her, she wavered between glorying in the men's upholding their honor and fearing the unknown path ahead.

On February 9, Jefferson Davis was elected President of the Confederate States of America. The town's own company, the Eufaula Rifles, was mustered into the service of the State of Alabama and prepared to leave as part of Davis's escort to Montgomery, where the Confederacy formed. Jonathan Ramsey, Harrison Wingate, and Edward Bullock were going also.

The twelfth had dawned brilliant with sunlight. Now as Emma stood on the porch, a balmy breeze blew, tantalizing with false spring as delightful as only February could be. Scarlet flowering quince and yellow daffodils emblazoned the street down which she watched people, brought out by the sonorous hum of the riverboat, pour forth in parade. Looking at the black puffs above the treetops, Emma had only one thought: *Jonathan is leaving.*

By the time she could brush her hair and fasten it with tortoiseshell combs, she heard the prancing feet of ponies and hurried out to climb into Lily's carriage. Even Lily had lost her voice. As they rode to the Pope home at the foot of Broad Street, their silence intensified the jingling of the reins.

Jonathan came to stand behind her under the huge oak tree. His breath was warm upon the back of her neck as Miss Ella Pope presented the colors to Eufaula Rifles' Captain Alpheus Baker. Jonathan smiled down at Emma with an odd light in his eyes as the speeches were made. When John Van Houten lifted his violin with soft, white hands and scraped his bow in a plaintive cry, she looked at Jonathan through a mist of tears and wondered why his expression had changed. Around her, women wept as the sorrowing violin unleashed their pent emotions. Jonathan brushed against her, and she drew a shaky breath.

When the ceremony ended, Jonathan lightly grasped her elbow in a tingling touch and helped her into the carriage. They rode slowly behind the soldiers as they marched to the wharf.

The tread of the marching men and the beat of their drums pounded in Emma's temples, and she could not think.

No laughter sparkled in Jonathan's eyes now as he looked at Emma's flushed cheeks. He cleared his throat and spoke haltingly. "Van Houten amazes me. Uh — has he — was he born blind?"

"No, um — I think he was . . ." Emma coughed and blinked back tears. She struggled to get her voice into its natural range. "He was fourteen — had sore eyes . . . The doctor's treatment — uh — destroyed his sight."

"I see." On the seat between them, his fingers brushed hers, twined, gripped. "What a pity . . ."

Emma swallowed. The warmth of his gaze and the softness of his voice made his words, to which neither was listening, float around her like a love song. She could feel her cheeks flaming in response to the pressure of his hand, and she looked quickly toward the front seat of the carriage. Lily's and Harrison's erect backs evidenced their endeavors to ignore them. Turning questioning eyes to Jonathan's face, she tried to continue speaking casually so as not to say the words of longing shouting from her heart. "He — he turned it for the good. He went to Weimar, Hungary, and studied under the great Franz Liszt . . ."

Uh! Uh! Uhmmm! The steamboat's mournful blast enveloped her. They had reached the end of the street. The carriage rolled by the Tavern. She sighed as they descended the hill and stopped at the wharf.

The steamer, *Ben Franklin,* waited impatiently, its boilers hiccupping steam. People were surging up the gangway, filling both

71

decks of the flat-bottomed boat, waving, shouting. The band struck up a tune and men hanging over the rails and women answering from the banks joined in lustily singing "Ben Bolt" and "Lily Dale." Many leading citizens were accompanying the soldiers on the first leg of the journey up-river to Columbus, Georgia.

Jonathan lifted Emma tenderly from the carriage. Saying nothing, he retained her hand and hurried her away from the crowd to a spot where the forest marched down to the muddy water.

The crisp breeze kissed her cheeks with color as she followed silently. Stepping into the cold shadow of a giant oak which sheltered them from prying eyes, she trembled violently.

Jonathan's strong arms enwrapped her. Weakly, she clung to him and relaxed against his warmth. He held her for a long, lingering moment. Gently, he pushed back the bonnet which shielded her face from him. He looked questioningly at her and then drew her close again and spoke lovingly with his lips against the golden ringlets escaping around her forehead. "Lovely Emma. Darling Emma. Why did I wait until I had to leave to realize I don't want to part from you? Everything has been moving so fast.

My duties are pressing . . ." He caressed her hair.

"Oh, Jonathan, Jonathan," she breathed. "I do understand," she whispered, gazing adoringly at his face, close above hers.

"I should have told you about —" he said earnestly. His face creased in a worried frown. "I want to ask you . . ." He ceased to struggle for words and said simply, "I need you."

Her smiling lips lifted to meet his. The tenderness of his kiss softened the last time-calloused edges of her heart.

Wheet! Wheet! A shrill whistle and white puffs of steam signaled last call.

"I must go." He held her away and gazed at her radiant face. "I'll return as soon as — you'll wait?"

"Forever." She smiled. The shroud of her fear fell from her. Straightening her bonnet, she stepped back into the sunshine of the river path with only a glimmer of a thought of how angry Cordelia would be if anyone had observed her scandalous behavior.

Jonathan ran up the gangway. It lifted. *Clang! Clang! Clang!* bells signaled importantly. Slowly the huge paddle wheel strained. Lifting a sparkling cascade of water, it strengthened into a rhythmic *swish,* swiftly propelling the steamboat away.

"I do declare, Emma," Lily greeted Emma, cocking her head to one side and laughing, "if I didn't know you were a lady, I'd say you had on rouge."

Emma's blush deepened, and her smile seemed to animate every inch of her body.

"Tell, tell!"

"He loves me," she sighed.

Lily squeezed her hand delightedly. Together, they looked across the intervening water at their men waving from the upper deck.

"I remember as if it were yesterday the first time I saw Harrison," said Lily softly. "We were sitting right here. He was so quiet and strong. In command of the situation."

Emma laughed. "And so totally inaccessible to you with your mother's demanding that you marry within your class," she said nodding. "And your vowing not to marry anyone unless he was a Christian."

"Oh, it does matter," Lily responded seriously. "When marriage is based on the love of God, your love just keeps on growing!" She frowned at Emma and said in a concerned tone which made her seem the elder. "What about Jonathan's faith?"

"I don't know." Emma stopped with a sudden flare of anger. Trying to shrug off the question, she concentrated on waving one last time before the white wake of the steamboat churned out of sight. From the corner of her eye, she could see by Lily's bowed head and clasped hands that she was praying. She knew Lily thought God cared about every detail of her life. Defiantly, she threw back her head and looked at the sky. Under her breath she queried, "If You do care about me, God, bring Jonathan back."

The kinswomen said little until they reached Barbour Hall. Then Emma asked haltingly, "When do you think they'll return?"

"I'm afraid it will be awhile. Didn't he tell you why they were going?"

"No."

"To organize a navy."

On Saint Valentine's Eve, Foy attended a party at Cordelia's prodding. Even though the tall, thin boy groaned and protested in a hoarse croak that it was silly to have to draw a name and be someone's valentine, Emma noticed a sly gleam in his eye. Smiling, she looked down from her bedroom window as he loped across the yard and realized that the years were passing and her small charge would soon be grown. She wondered if he had a special girl. Chuckling, she stood looking out at the moonlight patterning her lace curtains, remembering Ophelia's song from *Hamlet:*

Tomorrow is Saint Valentine's Day
All in the morning betime,
And I a maid at your window,
To be your Valentine.

Throughout the next morning, she stood idly with her hands poised over her tasks. Only when Cordelia began to eye her suspiciously did she realize that she was daydreaming as much as Lily once had. Late that afternoon, Emma noticed an envelope bearing her name placed in the card tray on the narrow, mahogany library table near the entrance doors. She opened the envelope with shaking fingers and lifted out a lovely bit of red satin and white lace. Clutching it to her heart, she ran up the stairs to her room before she looked at it and read the verse:

When first I saw thee,
Thy placid face,
With all the charms,
That play about it
I loved thee.
From J.

As the days passed without further word,

Emma occasionally climbed the stairs to the attic and rushed up the two more short flights to the belvedere. No telltale puffs of smoke appeared above the treetops to promise the arrival of a steamboat. Because she could hardly bear the closed feeling of the dark, narrow passageway and because the belvedere, with its three floor-to-ceiling windows front and back and two on each side, made her feel a bit dizzy, she abandoned the lookout and tried to keep busy. She removed the plumes of pampas grass which had decorated the parlor for the winter and went out into the side yard to cut forsythia branches and daffodils.

March was roaring in like a lion, and the wind whipped her hooped skirt and snatched her hair from the knot at the back of her neck. Intent upon shielding her basket of fragile, yellow flowers, she did not realize anyone had entered the garden until she looked up into the dark and laughing eyes of Jonathan Ramsey.

"Oh," she gasped with her free hand flying to her throat.

"I'm sorry I startled you," he apologized quickly. "You make such a picture that I hated to stop you. I wish I were a painter."

"The title would be 'Dishevelment,' no doubt," she returned wryly, dabbing futilely at her hair. "Come, let's see if the gazebo will give us a little shelter from the wind." Keeping a decorous distance between them, she led him to the white-latticed summerhouse. The octagon-shaped enclosure was festooned with gnarled wisteria vines, covered with limp buds, full of promise.

"Have you heard the exciting news?" he asked. Vibrant with enthusiasm, he seemed almost to dance from one foot to the other.

"No," she replied evenly. Placing her basket on the wicker and rattan table, she felt suddenly shy in his presence and chose to sit in one of the wicker chairs instead of on the double settee.

"The Confederate Navy is now formally constituted under the direction of Stephen Mallory." He strode back and forth, speaking in a voice pitched high with excitement. "We have sent peace emissaries to the United States with a formal demand to turn over Fort Sumter and Fort Pickens since they lie within our territory." Suddenly he stopped his pacing and stood before her. "With this show of strength, we will surely avert war."

She had never seen him this agitated. Emma sat quietly, while silence lengthened. She gazed up at him expectantly.

"Uh-um." He cleared his throat. "Now

that these affairs are settled," he resumed softly, "I feel that I can speak what is in my heart." He dropped to sit in the other wicker chair and scraped it across the marble floor until he was close beside her. His smooth face drooped with seriousness. In a doubtful tone he said, "I want to ask you to be my wife."

Emma's breath caught in her throat at the suddenness of his proposal. She opened her mouth, but words could not form; and her delicate face paled.

"No, wait." He waved a shushing hand. "Don't answer yet." His forehead creased with worry, and he swallowed before he continued. "There's something I should have told you — Would it matter to you terribly that — that I've had a wife?"

Emma gazed into his eyes, open wide like a wistful ten-year-old boy's, and smiled reassuringly. Ever so gently she brushed her fingertips across his smooth cheek and whispered, "No, that cannot affect the depth of my feelings for you."

Swiftly, he grasped both her hands in his, kissed them, then bowed his head upon them. "There's more. I have a child. A daughter."

"I know," she murmured. "Lily . . ."

"Of course. Then — dare I hope?"

"I love children," she said quietly, tenderly. "My arms have longed for one of my own . . ." Color rushed back into her cheeks.

His eyes searched her face. "Yes. Well . . . You see — Luther Elizabeth died when the baby came. I was devastated — I've wandered — I hardly know my child — she doesn't know me." Blinking back tears, he bowed his head upon her hands. "I promised myself that I would never fall in love again."

Pulling one hand free, she gently stroked his springing, dark curls until he raised his head and smiled happily. Catching her hand, he tenderly kissed the palm.

"You are so like my Betty, all pink and blue and gold with the wide-eyed innocence of a freshly scrubbed child." He chuckled.

Emma stiffened ever so slightly.

He hurriedly added, "Oh, no, I'll never compare you. You, dear Emma, are a caring woman. I enjoy your mind. I want to experience life with you."

Seeing how closely he was attuned to her feelings, she spoke confidently, "I do understand. At sixteen, in love with life — wanting to be in love — I thought I was terribly, painfully in love, but . . ." He was moving nearer and his breath was sweet and warm on her face. Pushing her hand against the rough material of his coat, she could feel his heart beating. "No, wait, I want to tell you — now that I've met you, I know what I felt then was not really love at all."

His arms closed around her, strong, warm, shielding her from the damp March wind. She met his kiss ardently, sealing their love.

"I know you'll want a proper period of engagement," he said at last, "but don't make me wait too long. I'm eager to take you to my plantation. It's in Bulloch County, Georgia, over near Savannah."

She nodded, too full of emotion to trust her voice. Shivering as the wind blew colder, knowing Cordelia would be looking for her, she reluctantly told him she must go.

As she entered the hall, Cordelia accosted her. "You're seeing entirely too much of that man!" She eyed her suspiciously. "Are his intentions honorable?"

Surprised, Emma blurted, "Why, yes, they are. He asked me to marry him," she said with unaccustomed sharpness.

Cordelia Edwards drew herself up with a haughty sniff. "Why — why, you know nothing of his background," she spluttered.

"I know enough," said Emma firmly between clenched teeth. Miserably, she wished she had not let her sister-in-law bully her into this admission before she could announce it joyfully.

Deflated, Cordelia sank to the horsehair sofa. Her voice a whine, she said, "But surely, you're not thinking of leaving me in my old age." She projected a pitiful, heavy lump, sliding down on the shiny, slick surface, but her next words carried an edge. "Not after all these years that I've provided you a good home."

Lily, of course, was delighted. On the fourth of March, the family, including Jonathan, went to the Wingate home on Eufaula Avenue. The modesty of the old, cottage-type house was characteristic of Harrison Wingate and reminded Emma of the way his humility had caused Cordelia to refuse him her daughter's hand because she had thought him a poor riverboat captain below their social strata. The small engagement party was proceeding with great gaiety until an agitated knock sounded at the door.

Harrison's face creased with deep lines of worry as he relayed to them the message from the telegraph office. Lincoln's inaugural address earlier that day had not answered the questions burning in Southern minds. "His wording casts serious doubt on the negotiations for peace," the tall man said, sadly shaking his head. "I believed with our leaders that when Lincoln saw us arming, he would surely back down and let us peacefully form our own nation."

With the spontaneity of the party spoiled, the guests departed early. When only the family remained, Foy turned to the captain, whom he idolized. "What will you do," he asked with owl-eyed seriousness, "if it comes to war? You didn't believe in dueling — would you fight in war?"

"Yes, Son," Harrison answered quietly. "I'll defend my home and my country."

"But–but," the boy stammered, "it's hard to understand." His ears turned red. "In the Old Testament, King David fought in wars, but in the New Testament — you always quote 'turn the other cheek'. . . ."

"From a personal insult, yes." Harrison rubbed the creases in his forehead. "Perhaps it will help you to turn in the Bible to Paul's letter to the Romans, especially chapter thirteen. He says, 'Let every soul be subject unto the higher powers.' Paul explains that government is ordained by God." He clapped Foy's shoulder. "And don't forget, he was saying this even though at the time the rulers were very evil."

The next weeks weighed their spirits with waiting. March scampered away like the proverbial lamb. As peace hung in the balance, Emma felt her own fate dangling.

"If there should be war," Jonathan declared solemnly one afternoon as they sat in the gazebo, "of course, we will have to postpone our wedding plans."

The wisteria, dripping off the gazebo in lavender cascades, filled the air with a heady fragrance that seemed to increase the ache in Emma's heart. Even though they would not have married anyway until after a proper period of engagement, the finality in his voice tightened her nerves.

"War. What a terrible word." She sighed. "And civil war — unthinkable."

He squeezed her hand and spoke reassuringly, "Even if there's war, it won't last long."

April unfolded gently, fluttering from her chrysalis with poetic beauty. Jonathan called for Emma in a runabout, and they drove along the Chattahoochee. Ferns and wildflowers crowded the narrow roadside. In the woodlands, wild azaleas flamed. Beneath tall trees, dogwoods stood in pristine beauty like diminutive brides in airy veils. Waiting.

They rode beneath the watercolor sky through lacy trees of gentle, yellow-green, their fingers twined on the red leather seat. The pleasant smell of freshly turned earth filled the air. Singing floated across the dell as field hands dropped cotton seed into the bright red clay waiting expectantly to burst forth with bounty. Occasionally Jonathan said amusing things, but Emma smiled wistfully because his eyes held a faraway look.

Cordelia fussed because Emma had gone out unchaperoned. Perturbed, Emma flared that she was hardly a debutante.

Then, on April 12, in Charleston Harbor, the thing they had been dreading happened. A gun thudded. A shell whined across a mile of water. War began. From the moment the news of the bombardment arrived, the men of the town remained milling about the telegraph office.

Surrender of Fort Sumter had been denied. Beauregard had fired the shot. By the next day, Major Anderson had surrendered the fort for the Union.

Emma sat at the rolltop ladies' secretary in her bedroom and recorded in her journal:

Great excitement prevails in Eufaula with the surrender of Fort Sumter. All communications between us and the North have stopped. Telegraph wires are pulled down and even the express news has been discontinued.
Preparations on both sides are being made for war.

Putting down her pen, she wept into her folded arms. She could not bear to write her anguish at what this might mean for Jonathan and her.

A few days later the cannon boomed again from the bluff, heralding celebration at the secession of Virginia.

A week after the Confederates took Fort Sumter, Lily bounded into Barbour Hall, shouting, "Emma, have you heard the terrible news?"

CHAPTER 6

"Terrible news?" Emma paused, open-mouthed. "What could be worse news than war?"

"Lincoln has blockaded our ports." Lily stamped her foot. "Our gateway to the world just clanged shut!"

"She's worried about no more Paris gowns," Harrison teased laughingly.

"Well, I do have a little sense," Lily flared, tossing her dark hair. "All we have around here is cotton, cotton, cotton. If we can't get manufactured goods or mineral resources from the North, they can't cut off our supplies from Europe . . . ," she snapped fierily.

Jonathan had come in behind them. *He always seems to catch me in a faded dress,* thought Emma ruefully. However, if he noticed her clothing he never commented. Nodding a greeting, he looked directly into her eyes and smiled dazzlingly.

"What we came to tell you, Emma, is . . . ," Jonathan's excitement seemed a tangible thing bouncing from wall to wall, "is — well, good-bye."

Emma's blue eyes widened in alarm. "What?"

"Oh, not for long," he continued quickly. "They've closed the biggest ports first. We're heading for Apalachicola as quickly as possible before they realize the importance of the Chattahoochee River."

"The *Wave* has been pressed into service for the Confederate Navy," explained Harrison in his usual quiet way.

With shaking hands, Emma began to set the cart for afternoon tea. She had just gathered a small pail of strawberries and whipped a bowl of cream to smother biscuits made flaky with a great deal of lard. As she worked, she surreptitiously searched Jonathan's face for signs of the wanderlust of which Lily had warned. He, himself, had told her that he had not planned to fall in love a second time. He almost danced as he helped her push the mahogany tea cart to the parlor where Cordelia Edwards waited beside a low fire. His movements showed Emma his eagerness for adventure.

Mrs. Edwards helped herself to an extra dollop of cream and said, "I know President

Lincoln and President Davis have both called for army volunteers —" She savored a bite of tart, juicy strawberries. "But do you think they'll actually go to war?"

"Yes, Miss Cordelia," replied Harrison. "I'm afraid both sides are as eager for battle as two young hotheads calling each other out for a duel."

"In fact, Ma'am," Jonathan added, "News of bloodshed came today. Seems there was a fight in Baltimore with the Seventh Regiment New York and a Boston company attempting to pass through the city on their way to Washington at Lincoln's command." He spread a square of white damask across his leg and grinned as he took a plate from Emma. "But don't you fret. This war will be as temporary as — as a napkin on a fat man's lap!"

War talk was forgotten as they laughed together and enjoyed their tea. Looking down at her hands, trembling as they lifted the silver teapot, Emma was struck for the first time by their bareness. She had given only passing thought to the fact that he had presented her with no token of betrothal; now, however, she could not stop staring at her bare hands. Bent on merrymaking, the men urged her across the hall to the music room. They lustily sang "Old Zip Coon,"

"Dan Tucker," "Oh, Susanna," and "Old Uncle Ned" while Emma played the grand piano with plain, bare fingers.

The next morning, April 20, Emma rode with Lily to the river. As they drove through the busy storehouse area, crowded with Saturday shoppers who had come into town from the surrounding cotton plantations, the women were forced to stop several times until wagons, loaded with provisions already becoming scarce, could pass. The steamboat's impatient whistle made Emma clutch nervously at her yellow plaid skirt.

Lily patted her. "Don't worry; Harrison wouldn't leave without saying good-bye."

Intense excitement surrounded the *Wave* as the stevedores loaded the last of the freight from the wharf. The tremendous, flat-bottomed boat, fully 175 feet long, was Harrison Wingate's pride and joy. Fire and black smoke belching from the two towering smokestacks told Emma the boilers must be fully stoked, ready to depart. The busy captain honored them by singling them out of the crowd, beaming and saluting them from the pilothouse. Some fifty-odd passengers, milling along the rails of both upper and lower decks, made a colorful blur; consequently, Emma could not distinguish which one was Jonathan. She focused on the gleaming, round paddle box emblazoned with the boat's name and, above that, her insignia, a painting of a descending dove. The huge water wheel beneath the paddle box seemed to shiver, as eager to leave as Jonathan. Shrieking whistles and clanging bells rasped Emma's nerves, and she wished she had not tried to say goodbye.

"I wish we were going with them," Lily declared as she led Emma up the gangway. Jonathan suddenly appeared beside them, and, with his touch, Emma's tension lifted. Elated that he had been watching for her, she smiled up at him, handsome in a doe-colored waistcoat and slim, dark trousers. Gaily, he tipped his top hat and whispered an endearment, causing both to laugh. They could hear nothing but the shouting of the roustabouts. He guided her to the upper deck and found a spot where the staterooms kept the wind from snatching at her fanchon. Pushing down the streamers of the bonnet, she noticed that Lily had gone to Harrison's cabin for a private farewell, for, of course, no emotion should be displayed in public.

Trying to smooth the anxiety and longing from her face, Emma stood as relaxed as possible, but her knuckles were white as she grasped the rail.

Inches away, Jonathan shifted from one foot to the other and lifted his hands toward her shoulders, then dropped them uncertainly. Under her yellow lace mantilla, the hairs on her arms tingled, and she shivered.

The mixed emotions on his face made her struggle for words to ease their tension. How she wished she could say she would miss him. Instead, she avoided his eyes, stared at his bright cravat, and heard herself saying, "Be careful. This river's so dangerous! The whirlpools —" She bit her lip. "The hidden obstructions . . . so many boats have sunk."

"Don't you worry." He laughed and smoothed the crease on her forehead with the tip of his index finger. "Wingate's had plenty of experience on this — what do they call it? The longest graveyard in the state of Georgia? But he knows where the hidden dangers lie." He bent closer and breathed sweetly against her face. "Don't you worry," he repeated tenderly as to a child.

His eyes twinkling, he lifted his head and laughed.

"Why, just the other day, Wingate was regaling the passengers with a story of a man who fell overboard several years ago. He was floundering and struggling in a swift current, calling loudly for help and 'bout to drown. Captain Wingate yelled from the pilothouse, 'Put your feet down! Stand up!' Finally the man did." Jonathan chuckled. "He was over a sandbar. The water was not waist deep!"

Laughing, Emma relaxed her tight fists and stood smiling at him radiantly.

"Emma, I — the war has interfered or I would have —"

Uhmmmmm! Uhmmmmm! The low growl of the whistle shook them. Passengers jostled for positions at the rail.

Hurriedly, Jonathan pulled a long narrow package from his waistcoat pocket and pressed it into her hand. A high piercing shriek signaled last call, and she could distinguish only, "a token" and "forget me."

"No, I'll never forget you," she whispered into the wind.

Lily hurried her ashore, where they watched the tremendous waterwheel on the side of the boat begin to turn. Dizzied by emotion, Emma wished for a share of the calm acceptance evident on Lily's face. Through swirling mists, Emma took one last look at Jonathan.

When they had climbed into the carriage, Emma opened the small package eagerly. Solemnly, she lifted a folded fan from the box and fingered the long, narrow ebony sticks, inlaid with gold. Slowly spreading the ribs apart, she held her breath for a long moment and looked at the beautiful painting on the soft, kidskin covering. With a long, shuddering sigh, she suddenly began to weep in shaking sobs.

"Why, it's exquisite! Whatever is the matter?" asked Lily in surprise.

"I expected —" Emma sniffed. "I hoped — it was a . . ." She began to cry again.

Clucking to the ponies, Lily slapped the reins and hurried them away. The open, fringe-topped carriage afforded no protection from curious eyes. "You're disappointed in the gift?" she inquired after they had moved beyond the crowd around the Tavern.

"No, no, it's more than that." Drooping dejectedly, Emma dried her face on the lace mantilla. "He said a token — not to forget him. He hasn't given me anything to seal the engagement. From the shape of the box, I'd hoped this was a necklace."

They rode up Barbour Street in silence. Then Emma continued brokenly, "He said he wanted to marry me — to take me to his plantation, but then — but then —"

"The war. And, yes, I can answer that

94

question in your eyes. He likes to move about."

"But if he'd just wanted a mother for his child — most men marry the first wife's sister or kinswoman . . ."

Concern showed in Lily's dark eyes. For once, she seemed at a loss for words.

Forlorn, Emma refused to attend church with Lily the next day; however, at ten o'clock Monday morning, she did go with her to the citywide prayer meeting. The business houses closed and some nine hundred people crowded into the church as the Reverends Cotton, Reeves, and McIntosh, representing various denominations, led in meditation and prayer to God in behalf of their beloved country.

Emma suppressed her cross mood with difficulty, remaining tensely silent during the long afternoon of assisting Cordelia's entertainment of her callers, Mrs. John Shorter and Mrs. Eli Shorter. The visit of Elizabeth Rhodes and her twin sister, Mollie Simpson, friends her own age, helped Emma relax a bit. But when Mrs. Dent and her daughter Lizzie bustled in, flushed and excited from a day in town shopping for Lizzie's upcoming wedding, Emma's throat constricted. A heavy lump in her chest and a throbbing headache made pleasant responses difficult.

"You'll just die when you see my bridal gown, Emma," Lizzie gushed. "You are coming out to the wedding, now?" she urged as they left for Fendall Hall to spend the night with the Edward Youngs.

"Yes," Emma answered quietly, "if I can get a ride."

Emma felt quite sick the next morning and was glad to get out of the house into the crisp morning air to gather strawberries. The melancholy which had hovered around her over the past days had gone unnoticed because every woman in town was saddened by departing soldiers.

She could not discuss her problems with Lily because Mignonne was running a high fever, and Lily sat bathing the child's brow and consulting in worried tones with Dr. Thornton during his several visits. Doggedly, Emma attended the frequent prayer meetings for their country with Cordelia, but she merely sat with clenched teeth, unable to pray, finding no comfort.

When Lizzie's wedding day, May 2, 1861, dawned cloudy and unpleasantly cold after April's summery heat, Emma's spirits sank lower. Her head ached and a slight sniffle made her wonder if she could stay at home, pleading a cold.

A quick footstep on the front porch caused her to catch her breath and look up from where she knelt adding a finishing touch to the arrangement of poppies and larkspur on the wall shelf in the receiving hall. Knowing Kitty had gone upstairs to help Cordelia dress for the wedding, she did not hold back her emotion. Her feet scarcely touched the black-and-white marble as she flung herself across the room and into Jonathan's outstretched arms. Crushed against him, unable to breathe, Emma let her hopes soar. The ardor of his kiss seemed to say that the separation had also been difficult for him.

Discreetly, she led him into the parlor where they could enjoy a moment of privacy. When she told him of John Horry Dent's daughter's wedding, he declared himself delighted to be her escort.

Her cold forgotten, she bounded up the stairs two at a time like Foy. Hurriedly, she donned a frock of pink organdy, with five tiers of flounces fluttering around the skirt and yet another ruffle across the bodice and sleeves. Did she look too much like Mignonne? Turning anxiously toward the cheval glass, she breathed a pleased sigh and smiled at her image. With her pink cheeks and unlined face, she did look young enough to be a bride herself. Radiantly, she descended the stairs to be met by Jonathan's smile of approval at the fluffy pink cloud around her.

Because Harrison had not returned and Lily chose not to leave her sick baby, Cordelia rode alone in the backseat of the carriage to the Dent plantation. But Jonathan answered Mrs. Edwards's grumpy questioning about his family background with patience and good humor.

The sun smiled forth upon the assembled Bleak House Plantation guests. Lizzie Dent, serenely lovely, emerged in a gown of lustrous white satin, made for her in New York several months before. As she and Whitfield Clark ex-changed vows, Emma stole glances at Jonathan; surely he would see weddings need not be postponed because of war.

Afterward, as they mingled with the guests on the festive grounds, Emma realized that the subject of the war crept into every conversation. *Men,* she sighed, *were less readily affected by beauty and love.*

John Horry Dent stood in the yard with a group of farmers. As Emma and Jonathan approached, she heard him saying in his slow, deliberate way, "As our country is at war, I'm thinking I should plant less cotton and more corn and provisions."

Others nodded and someone agreed, "Yes, we'll not be importing corn, and flour, and bacon for a while."

While they sat eating their barbecue, succulent pork swimming in the Dents' secret sauce, young Horry Dent came over to talk navy with Jonathan.

"Secretary Mallory has ordered me to New Orleans for duty on the steamer *McRea*," Horry said.

"You'll be under Captain Rosseau," returned Jonathan in a congratulatory tone. "Fine man. He'll know how to run the blockade."

"Yes," replied the smooth-cheeked young man seriously. "The Mississippi is where the important naval battles will be fought."

"Maybe," drawled Jonathan, "but I think I can find enough excitement on the Chattahoochee." He gave Emma a broad wink.

On the ride back into Eufaula that evening, Emma's emotions fluttered from the romance of the day. She felt certain Jonathan would ask to marry her before he returned to duty. She smiled up at him, handsome in his naval officer's uniform. A glance over her shoulder rewarded her with a view of Cordelia's nodding head. A snore indicated she was dozing, but Jonathan continued a noncommittal banter. Sighing, Emma tried to enjoy merely being in his presence. She contented herself with the promise in his wink.

But Jonathan left as suddenly as he had appeared, and Emma remained a spinster, joining other women as they waited for an occasional furloughed soldier or sailor to return. Lonely, uneventful days passed slowly. Cucumbers, beans, peas, and squash busied their hands, while Emma's mind winged along the river. Was Jonathan entertaining some other wide-eyed innocent girl with his stories?

On an afternoon in late May, Elizabeth Rhodes and Mollie Simpson called with exciting news. A dispatch had come from downriver that the U.S. warship, *Crusader,* was sailing toward the bay, with the express purpose of recapturing a schooner taken by the people of Apalachicola and burning the city. A company of fifty men left, taking all Eufaula's ammunition to help at the batteries being erected on Saint Vincent's Island to defend the bay. Fearfully the women waved as they steamed away.

Emma felt as limp as a bedsheet hung on a line, parched by the sun, whipped by the wind, as she waited for news of Jonathan. None came.

The soft, warm beauty of June went unnoticed. Business was nearly suspended as people waited for word of the war. Anxious lookouts watched the river from belvederes and cupolas, fearful that the enemy might break through the defenses at Apalachicola Bay and come steaming up the Chattahoochee.

On Mignonne's first birthday, June 11, 1861, Lily climbed, over and over, to the belvedere to scan the sky, stubbornly maintaining that Harrison would come to join in the celebration. Only after dark when her sleepy child could stay awake no longer, did Lily give up and wish her daughter a happy birthday. On noon of that day, they later learned, the screw steamer USS *Montgomery* had sealed the entrance to their port.

On June 13, the townspeople filled the churches in answer to President Davis's request that the Confederate States observe a day of fasting and prayer. Emma chafed at the inactivity of the long Thursday, quieter even than a usual Sabbath.

Business resumed slowly with people soberly admitting that they were in for a long and bloody siege. Too long, they now realized, they had been solely agricultural, depending upon the North for everything else. Confidence was still voiced by some that the South could win — if the war did not last too long.

Emma joined eagerly the newly organized Ladies' Aid Society, anxious to do any small thing she could to speed this conflict to a swift conclusion. Mrs. B. F. Treadwell had personally outfitted the first soldiers leaving Eufaula. Now more help was needed. Their neighbor, Mrs. L. L. Cato, accompanied by Mrs. Alpheus Baker, called at Barbour Hall to solicit contributions for the boys at the front. A few days later, Captain Baker himself, home on leave from Fort Pickens at Pensacola, Florida, spoke to the society, telling them what they needed to do first. Mr. Young donated meeting rooms above his store, and work began in earnest. Even though cutting and sewing heavy pants was exhausting, Emma relished the satisfaction of helping and went to the sewing rooms whenever Cordelia could spare her.

On Sunday the sky blazed with the tail of a comet, and moanings and whisperings about evil omens filled the servants' quarters. The comet gave Emma no cause to fear; but the next day, a small envelope bearing her name caused her to clutch both hands to her chest, almost too afraid to reach out and take it from the library table by the front door. A cryptic note, hurriedly scribbled in pencil, read:

Apalachicola Bay
June 12, 1861

My dear, sweet Emma,
    Blockade a farce. Painted my schooner and slipped right through. A neutral ship was outside the Sound with a special prize I had been expecting.
    See you soon as a cat can wink his eye.
My love,
J.

Time passed slowly. Emma helped cut soldiers' coats and paid a social call with Cordelia on Mrs. John Gill Shorter, at home from Montgomery, the state capital, where Eufaula's own Mr. Shorter was governor. During the last few weeks, she told them, since the moving of the capital of the Confederate States of America from Montgomery to Richmond, Virginia, changes had been brought about.

When, on a Monday morning, church bells began to toll, Emma rushed into the street to join the throng heading for the telegraph office. Rumors had spread the day before, at church, that a tremendous battle was taking place.

The clerk cleared his throat and began to read the dispatch, "Night has closed on a hard-fought field called Manassas. After a day-long battle, our forces are in possession of the field after a glorious victory."

Cheers rang out. The clerk stood waiting with his paper shaking with excitement.

"The numbers engaged were 35,000 Federals. The enemy was routed. They fled, abandoning a large amount of arms, munitions, knapsacks, and baggage."

Cheers interrupted him again.

"The ground is strewn for miles," his voice changed timbre, "with those killed. Confederates killed number 385. Federal dead estimated to be 450–500. The farmhouses are filled with wounded, 1500 Confederates and 1100 Federals."

A hush fell over the crowd as he continued to read praise for the gallantry of the troops and the resolution offered by the Confederate Congress. "We deplore the necessity which has washed the evil of our country with the blood of so many of her noble sons. We offer their families our warmest, cordial sympathy. . . ."

Emma turned away, but she could not shut out his words, "a dozen of our men have been captured. We have taken 1300 prisoners." Walking slowly toward home, she heard snatches, "Recognize the hand of the great high God . . . Sabbath service of thanksgiving and praise . . ." Before this, the war had been mere skirmishes with only an occasional man killed. Suddenly the specter of death loomed large.

Celebrations continued for this major victory. More messages brought the news that many people from Washington City had gone out to watch the battle in the Virginia village of Manassas, twenty-five miles southwest of the capital, for a Sunday excursion, and to cheer their attacking combatants with the cry, "On to Richmond!" General Thomas Jackson's brigade held firm, so firm that, in the afternoon, when General B. E. Bee arrived with reinforcements he declared, "There is Jackson standing like a stone wall." The Federals were driven back across a small river called Bull Run; and the spectators fled, with the new knowledge that the war would be more than one brief battle.

That afternoon, black puffs of smoke preceded the signal from the whistle of the *Wave*. The resulting happy reunion caught up even Cordelia in the excitement. It was decided that the family would attend the cotillion victory celebration.

Surveying her meager wardrobe in the walnut armoire, Emma sniffed disgustedly.

She would have to wear the same pink organdy she had worn to Liz's wedding. Cordelia magnanimously offered her a valuable pair of dangling earrings of Etruscan gold. Even though the style was currently popular, Emma decided they did not flatter her and declined.

When they arrived at the hotel on Broad Street, a crowd of men gathered around Harrison and Jonathan for news of the blockade. Emma greeted the other ladies vaguely, straining to hear the men's conversation.

"Why, the blockade's a farce," laughed Jonathan. "The Federals sent in a 787-ton screw steamer, the USS *Montgomery*." He chuckled. "How they ever thought they'd get something so huge in that shallow bay, I'll never know. Like trying to float a watermelon in a saucer." He grinned, and was rewarded by laughter from the crowd. "They tried to sound the water, but the ship almost ran aground," he continued. "They finally brought her into position. They do command the main entrance to the port."

"But they can't lock us in with oceangoing vessels, and they don't have any shallow-draft steamers — yet," added Harrison. "We can still slip our schooners through the shoal water because their big screw propellers can't maneuver in the narrow, intricate channels. They'll never apprehend all our blockade runners since there are four passages to watch at once."

"You know how the semicircle of islands separates Apalachicola from the Gulf of Mexico," Jonathan continued.

Emma leaned forward, aware that he was drawing with his finger, but uncertain of what he was outlining.

"They have blocked West Pass between Sand Island and Saint Vincent's Island and stopped neutral ships from standing off Saint Vincent's Bar to be relieved of cargo by the lighters from the wharves. But!" He waved his index finger and continued gleefully, "We can still slip through Indian Pass between Saint George Island and Indian Peninsula and — well, just the other night I made it through East Pass between Saint George and Dog Island."

Awed murmurings hummed over the group of men.

"But how can you stay clear of the *Montgomery*'s guns?" queried Foy, shouldering his way into the crowd as Emma wished she could do.

"By a simple trick," Jonathan replied. His dancing eyes met Emma's over Foy's shoulder, but he continued his story, "I painted my little schooner, the *Hollycock,* white."

"White?" chorused the men. "Not black?"

"No. A dull white. Properly painted, she is absolutely indiscernible at a cable's length. Of course, all the crew must wear white at night. One black figure on the bridge would betray an otherwise invisible vessel. Not even a cigar is allowed."

A thrill of vicarious excitement stirred the less daring.

"The *Hollycock* is an extremely fast sailor." Jonathan was enjoying playing to an audience now, and he warmed to his story. "She has a very low hull and slender spars that make her particularly hard to see in darkness. On foggy or moonless nights, we lower her sails and drift with the current right past the blockaders." Grinning, he paused in his story as the listeners nodded and laughed, visualizing the daring of his scheme. "Time and again we've eluded detection. Even though we could see the blockaders, they couldn't see us. But the other night," exhilaration vibrated in his voice, "we had cotton in every space — bales even in the cabin and —"

"Is it true," Foy interrupted breathlessly, "that you scatter a few barrels of oil in the hull and connect a fuse in case — in case of capture?"

"Yes." Jonathan nodded. "We couldn't let so valuable a cargo fall into the hands of the enemy. We'd have to burn it. Anyway," he continued his story, "the moon came from behind a cloud just as we drifted by, and the lookout spotted us. The *Montgomery* steamed in pursuit. We ran up our canvas, but we lacked the speed to outrun them."

Ears pricked, Emma leaned forward, not caring if it was unladylike to join the group of men who were now hushed expectantly.

"Suddenly the wind becalmed. Their bullets played 'Ole Dan Tucker' around my ears." He paused and smiled with every eye upon him. "It seemed we were lost."

"What happened?" several chorused.

"A great gust filled her sails. We ran for shore seeking the safety of the shoals. The *Hollycock* is a centerboard schooner. That means that an adjustable blade, pushed out through her flat-bottomed keel, maintains her perpendicular. We drew up the centerboard to reduce the draft." He shrugged his shoulders, expressing ease. "Went right over a bar in only four and a half feet of water . . ." He motioned outwardly with both hands. The men guffawed at the image of the big steamer's being foiled.

"On the Atlantic," Harrison said, "blockade-running is a science. Here on the

Gulf, it's a gentleman's game."

Emma turned away at the sound of their laughter. Jonathan had described his exploits as though he had been running his yacht in the America's Cup race. The sudden realization of danger sickened her.

Sawing scrapes on the violin as the orchestra tuned up made Emma wince as she stumbled across the room blinded by tears. The tune of a cotillion filled the ballroom, and many couples joined in the brisk dance. Emma sat miserably on the sidelines. Still surrounded, Jonathan continued to talk. When the cotillion ended, Van Houten tapped his baton and indicated three lively beats. Emma smiled as they struck up the lilting "Tallahassee Waltz." Hidden by her hoop skirt, her feet began to dance in place.

Jonathan bowed before her. With twinkling eyes, he said, "Our waltz is becoming very popular. It's such a light and dainty tune that the moment I hear it, I think of you." He took her hand and led her to the floor. Danger was forgotten.

At first, her toes tripped instead of gliding, and the flounces of her pink organdy fluttered as her hooped skirt rocked upward, forward to the right, forward to the left. The steadying of his hands made her relax. She glided smoothly in the backward steps and began to float on the joyful rhythm of three-quarter time.

Laughing, flushed after several Strauss waltzes, Emma begged for air. Jonathan led her from the heat of the ballroom to a corner of the veranda where a cool breeze wafted the fragrance of honeysuckle. Other couples crowded the porch and there was little privacy; but the tenderness of his face as he gazed at her made her feel she had been kissed.

"I told you I captured a special prize," said Jonathan, like a little boy who had just caught Santa Claus. "I'd sent a message home — I'd been waiting . . ." He took out a long, narrow package shaped like the one that had held the fan and pressed it into her hand.

With shaking fingers, she lifted the top of an ebony box. Sparkling against the white velvet lining, a necklace of rubies cast a pink glow. She drew a deep breath. "Oh, it's so lovely," she gasped. "Oh, I never expected to have anything so beautiful!"

"You grow more beautiful every time you smile." His face shone with candid emotion.

Emma could not resist brushing his smooth cheek with her fingertips.

"I'm glad you're wearing pink tonight."

He laughed softly, as if slightly embarrassed at the tremor in his voice. "The first time I saw you, you had on pink velvet. Your radiance made me think of the pink rubies which belonged to my mother," he said gently as he took the necklace from the box in her hand and fastened it about her slender neck.

Unable to speak, she pressed the cool jewels against her porcelain skin and looked at him through misted eyes.

"I wanted to wait for the perfect gift for you — one that would have special meaning." His voice was tender as his eyes held hers for a long moment before he added laughingly, "but I almost lost it when the Yankees blocked the port." Lifting a matching ruby ring from the box, he slipped it on her finger. Grasping her hand tightly, he whispered, "You haven't changed? You'll still be mine?"

"Oh, Jonathan, of course," she breathed. "Always." With shining eyes, she looked up at him. "You know — I'm sure you do — that I have little dowry — I couldn't have a fine wedding, but I'm sure the Reverend Reeves will . . ."

Jonathan dropped her hands and grasped the porch rail. "Emma —" He hesitated. "Dearest Emma, please understand. I don't want to risk . . ."

Her lashes fanned back from anxious eyes.

"I didn't mean this for a wedding gift. I can't marry you now. I must leave." His voice cracked. He swallowed hard. "I just meant this to pledge our engagement. Please understand," he repeated. "The C.S.A. is dependent upon people like me to slip through the blockade."

"People like you!" Her voice rose shrilly and her lower lip trembled. "You're a worse daredevil than that hot-air balloonist who came through. You risked your life for these rubies and then — and then . . ." She flung out her hand and the hard stone clanked against the column. "I thought you'd finished your childish adventuring. Blockade-runners —" The necklace followed the heaving of her chest.

"Blockade-runners are f–f–foolhardy!" she sobbed.

CHAPTER 7

Jonathan drew back red-faced. Glancing at the other couples, he took the weeping woman by the elbow, led her off the porch, and hurried her down the walk. Pushing her behind the shelter of a thick magnolia, he stood apart from her, stiff with anger and embarrassment.

Burying her face in her hands, she sobbed uncontrollably.

"Don't," he whispered miserably, "please, don't!"

"Why must you continue to take such foolish chances?" she snuffled. "Cotton bales can stay in a w–w–warehouse. We can do without Paris gowns and Italian marble."

"Is that what you think?" he spat out disgustedly. "Maybe I did risk my life for your jewels — which you don't seem to appreciate — but . . ."

"Oh, Jonathan, of course I do!" She wailed and clutched the necklace in both hands, "I love my — my engagement gifts. It — it seemed so much that I thought it was — a wedding gift — I misunderstood." She gulped. Forlornly, she dropped her head.

Gently, he kissed the golden curls on the top of her bowed head.

"I'm so ashamed!" Her words wavered on a sigh. "I'm frightened."

"Little one, don't cry." Jonathan enfolded her in his arms and stroked her hair as she wept into the rough gray material of his uniform. "I understand," he whispered. "I know your friends are marrying, but . . . I don't want to risk — leaving you in — a family way — alone . . ."

Emma snuggled in the tight circle of his arms and dabbed at her eyes. "I wouldn't be alone. Lily's here . . . you're here often. I'm not afraid of — that . . ."

He pulled her roughly against his chest and buried his face in her hair. "I saw Betty die. Be patient with me, Emma." He hugged her convulsively. "Please wait 'til I'm here to stay."

Almost unable to breathe, she sighed. "Oh, Jonathan, I'll wait." She raised her lips for a lingering kiss to seal their betrothal.

"I want you to understand," he said at last. He guided her to a bench in the garden and began to explain. "The cotton in the warehouses in Apalachicola alone is worth a million dollars even if you only count it ten cents a pound." He held both her hands in his and continued urgently. "What you must realize is that everyone in southwest Georgia and southeast Alabama is entirely dependent upon the sale of cotton for the necessities of life. Cotton is the only thing the Confederacy can sell for gold or trade for weapons of defense!"

Drooping dejectedly, Emma looked at her hands and said nothing.

Jonathan continued in a strained voice. "The South has few factories. Our soldiers have few arms except what they can capture. We are sealed off from our supplies of guns and ammunition from Europe. We *must* run the blockade!"

"Yes," she sighed. "I see what you mean, but — you're not a sailor. Can't someone else . . . ?" She pulled her hands from his and clenched and unclenched fistfuls of pink organdy ruffles. "I thought you were a farmer."

Jonathan laughed halfheartedly. "I'm learning. The Confederate Navy has outstanding officers. Many resigned their commissions in the United States Navy. We have many British naval officers, the very cream of the English Navy, who have temporarily become captains of blockade-runners. Perhaps the rest of us are farmers — but we are learning."

The moon was high, and many of the older people were leaving. Emma stirred uneasily, knowing Cordelia would be looking for her. Jonathan rose slowly, as if he were carrying a heavy weight, and smiled sadly down at her. She felt too weak-kneed to stand.

"The Confederacy must have cloth for uniforms — buttons, thread, boots, shoes, stockings," he said disgustedly, "iron, steel, copper, chemicals — medicines — salt. Can't you comprehend that I must . . ."

"Yes. Yes, I see. I'll wait for our wedding."

She gave him her hand. Silently they rejoined the dancers, but the melody seemed muted. Emma accepted compliments on her jewels and congratulations from Lily, Elizabeth, and Mollie; but her heart felt as cold as the glitter of the rubies.

Wait. Wait. Wait. The cruel word pounded often in her temples in tandem with a raging toothache, complicated by several trips to the dentist. Dr. Plant filled the offending cavity, but an ulceration at the root necessitated his removing the filling. Pacing her room, holding a rock heated in the fireplace against her cheek, she agonized over her silly behavior as much as over the pain in her mouth. She must not rush Jonathan to marry her or she would surely drive him from her.

Her love and yearning for him had grown stronger, but he had drawn away. Did his distant attitude indicate that he regretted his proposal? She flung the rock into the coals. He had said he needed her. He had never actually voiced the words of love she longed to hear. Hot tears of pain and anguish burned down her cheeks.

The Confederates were trying to reinforce their hold upon Apalachicola from the batteries on Saint Vincent's Island, but their supply of guns and ammunition was pitifully small. Emma did not try to discuss her resulting fears with Lily — who was totally enthralled with teaching Mignonne to walk.

The post office was still receiving mail by stage; she checked daily, fruitlessly, for a letter from Jonathan. An unusual amount of rain for August further dampened Emma's spirits. She spent the gray days straining her eyes over the stitching of soldiers' trousers. Working with the Ladies' Aid Society busied her hands, but her mind seemed deadened, and she stabbed her needle with a growing sense of hopelessness.

September shimmered in on a blast of dry heat. And with its bright sunshine, Emma's heart brightened with the sound of the pulsating whistle of the *Wave*.

The dining room of Barbour Hall was the site of as festive a meal as Emma could prepare with growing shortages. Despite Mrs. Edwards's remonstrations, Foy could not wait for polite dinner conversation and pestered the men until they revealed what had been happening.

"Well," grinned Jonathan, generously helping himself to Emma's freshly dug sweet potatoes, "it has been pretty exciting. We continued to slip by the *Montgomery* with no trouble, but the USS *R. R. Cuyler's* joining her tripled the number of men and guns against us."

Foy's reddened ears seemed to quiver as he held his fork in midair and leaned forward.

"The *Cuyler* is another screw steamer — the Union still doesn't have vessels suitable for operation in shallow water. On the night of August 26 . . ." Jonathan's voice became low and deliberate as it always did when he was spinning tales. "Five Yankee boats went out on reconnaissance from the *Cuyler* and *Montgomery* and discovered the supply ship *Finland* and the schooner *New Plan* at anchor in the bay." Jonathan took a bite of fried chicken and smiled at Emma in a way that communicated only his pleasure in the meal — nothing more to ease the slight restraint between them.

"Did they get away?" Foy croaked.

"No," contributed Harrison evenly. "The Yankees captured both of them easily. They made the crew of the *New Plan* take an oath of allegiance to the United States and then released them. They took the *Finland* as a lawful prize, but the Union seamen had trouble trying to remove their prize from the bay." He laughed and his eyes fastened on Lily's face in that special way in which they seemed to exchange thoughts. "The winds and tides were unfavorable, but the Federals attempted to tow the *Finland* to the blockading station at East Pass." He paused and grinned. "She grounded on Saint Vincent's Bar."

"And there she stayed all night 'til we came along about dawn." Jonathan gestured with his chicken leg. "The night was dark but dangerously clear. All hands were on deck. The sails were down, of course, and we were crouching behind the bulwarks when . . ."

Emma's attention had been on passing hot biscuits. Staring wide-eyed at Jonathan, she set the plate down with a *whack.*

Turning toward her, he explained, "Harrison, in the *Wave,* was towing my schooner, *Hollycock.* We were creeping down the river heading into Apalachicola. We had no lights. Not a sound could be heard save the regular *beat, beat, beat* of the paddle wheels which, in spite of our snail's pace, was dangerously loud."

"I was in the pilothouse, straining my eyes in the darkness," Harrison picked up the story, "when I saw the dim white outline of the surf. Suddenly, Burrus gripped my arm and pointed to the *Finland* on our starboard bow . . ."

"I had nine men from the Apalachicola Guards on the *Hollycock.* A centerboard schooner can pivot and navigate small circles with ease. We came around and fired a broadside." Jonathan chuckled with glee. "You should've seen those Yankees scatter. They set fire to the *Finland* and took to their boats."

"You mean you routed the Union Navy with only nine men?" Foy clapped his hands. "Nine men and courage! I've got to go with you next time!"

A snort of alarm came from Cordelia, who had been eating while the others talked.

Jonathan laughed. "We sent 'em running.

Didn't even injure one — but we hurt their pride! And we got back our supplies," he continued quickly. "Our detachment boarded the burning *Finland* and recovered the lifeboats, salvaging two hundred sacks of coffee, four hundred revolvers, a number of rifles, dirks, a six-pounder fieldpiece, five hundred thousand percussion caps, and a quantity of fruit."

"And the Yankee ships were too big to enter the bay and stop you?" Lily asked.

"Yes, Ma'am. We got away from them one more time." Jonathan patted his full stomach in satisfaction.

Emma twisted the ruby ring on her finger and asked timidly, "You look so tired. Can you stay awhile?"

"Wish we could." Harrison shook his head. "We must leave tomorrow morning for Columbus. This load must get to the supply lines. Low water will prevent our reaching Columbus before long."

"Have you heard much talk," Jonathan inquired, "about Columbus's being the nucleus of the Confederate Ordnance Department?"

"Columbus?" squeaked Foy, surprised that the nearby Georgia town was of any importance to the war.

"Yes," Lily interjected, "I'd heard it called

the largest industrial center south of Richmond. And since it's connected by railroad with Montgomery, Atlanta, and Richmond . . ."

"Sometimes I think this war's being waged by railroad men," grumbled Harrison bitterly. "The Union's choking off the waterways and laying rails."

"I'm going with you," said Lily suddenly. "A trip on the *Wave* is always such fun, and it looks like the only chance to see you."

Harrison smiled and nodded assent. "It will be a quick trip. I'll pick up a load of uniforms and tents from the cotton mills, and fifes and drums from the music store . . ."

"Please go by the mill and get me a barrel of meal and a barrel of flour," interrupted Cordelia.

Emma could not subdue the lights dancing in her eyes. Remembering how Lily and Harrison's romance had blossomed on the beautifully appointed steamboat with the orchestra playing and moonlight dancing upon the water, she held her breath, smiled shyly up at Jonathan, and asked softly, "Are you going, too?"

Jonathan's tone indicated the seriousness of his business. "Yes, I'm going to the Naval Ironworks to confer with Chief Engineer

Warner about getting some vessels built to move down the river and raise the blockade. We must work quickly before the Federals ascend the river and attack Columbus." A frown pursed his usually jolly face. "They know of the swords, rifles, and ammunition produced there. We only hope they don't know we're building a torpedo boat."

Emma slumped in her chair, toying with her food. Jonathan was too worried about defending the river to consider her. Powerless to go or do unless she was told, she leaned her head back against the tall chair.

"I've heard that with so many industries running day and night, even some women are working," said Lily, obviously fired with enthusiasm. "I wish I could do something useful."

"Lily!" Cordelia Edwards exclaimed and fanned herself in shock.

Lily laughed and finally caught Emma's pleading glance. "Um, Mama, why don't you and Emma come along and visit Aunt Laurie?"

Emma dared not breathe or look at her sister-in-law.

"Well, maybe," Mrs. Edwards replied slowly. "If you'll have done with foolish talk."

Hurried preparations were made for the

trip. Even though Cordelia feared wrecks from snags, obstructions in the shallow river, or fires from boiler explosions, the luxuries of water travel on a floating hotel such as the *Wave* and the anticipation of seeing her sister finally outweighed the dangers. All was in readiness when Foy caused an explosion of his own.

Standing by the front doors amid trunks and carpetbags, Foy declared, "I've packed all my belongings, Mama. I won't be coming back," he mumbled, head down and eyes averted. Suddenly, his chin came up with a defiance which equaled Lily's fire. "I'm joining the navy!"

"No!" Cordelia shrieked. "You're still a baby! You can't go." Then she whined, "You can't leave me."

Cordelia's shouts and cries during the carriage ride to the wharf proved to no avail. Foy's mind seemed made up.

Emma sat wringing her hands, allowed no voice in the destiny of this child she loved so much. She had watched him fearfully of late as many of his friends, lured, no doubt, by the colorful, braid-trimmed boleros and bloused Turkish trousers copied from French light-infantry uniforms, joined Brannon's Zouaves. Foy had even secured a *kepi.* She had seen him wearing the cap, running, and pretending to shoot from behind bushes.

With nothing resolved, they reached the wharf. Even though he was extremely busy, Captain Wingate was summoned. Although she always hated to admit her son-in-law's merits, Cordelia turned to him in despair.

"Wait a little, son," said Harrison with quiet firmness.

"I'm old enough! I've heard of drummer boys as young as ten," Foy flared defiantly.

"Yes." Harrison nodded. "You're right, but to become a midshipman you must be proficient in reading, writing, and the rudiments of mathematics. I'll help you every time I'm home. If you hope to be a naval officer, you must continue your schooling until you're sixteen."

"You promise I can go then?"

Harrison held out his hand and nodded solemnly.

Foy looked him in the eye and shook hands. Then he ducked his head to hide tears.

Cordelia sat down heavily, moaning, "Emma, we cannot travel. Foy has given me a brow ague! Unload the trunks. We'll go back home."

Emma's forehead dropped to her fist. Squeezing her eyelids, she realized she would not even be able to say good-bye to Jonathan. Sick with disappointment but knowing she was dependent upon Cordelia for a home, she had no choice but to obey.

"Summon Kitty and help me to bed," Cordelia ordered. "Then get me thirty grains of quinine."

Emma well knew that while the cure for Cordelia's aching head was taking its slow effect, she would be in no condition to supervise the many servants, to instruct and reinstruct them at each task. Emma was accustomed to running the household on these occasions while the quinine caused her sister-in-law to lose her equilibrium. Cordelia would clutch her head as if to ascertain its size and declare it filled with a dozen drums and roaring ocean waves. Although Emma did not taste the dose of quinine upon her own tongue, a bitterness filled her mouth, invaded her brain, spoiled her countenance, and stiffened her movements.

Early in October, when Elizabeth rushed in bubbling with the news that Mollie had delivered a son, Emma went with her to the magnificent, towering, three-and-a-half-story, Italianate mansion that William Simpson had built for his wife, Mary Ann, affectionately called Mollie, on North Randolph Street next to the home of her sister, Mrs. Chauncey Rhodes. The sisters had even had double weddings and, as Elizabeth tenderly bathed Mollie's face, Emma felt shut out by the twins' closeness and her own spinsterhood.

In the nursery, Mollie's three little girls crowded around her as she lifted William Thomas Simpson, Jr., in her arms. Pressing the tiny body to her heart and kissing his soft, sweet head, Emma was overwhelmed with longing.

Waiting on Mollie and holding the precious bundle became a daily joy and torment. As Emma walked back to Barbour Hall through the Indian summer afternoons with her skirt sweeping the dry, rustling leaves around her, she ached with the knowledge of her age — twenty-eight. Would Jonathan ever decide the time was right to marry? He never spoke of his daughter. Possibly he did not want other children.

Shrinking into a lonely shell, Emma made excuses to stop going to choir practice. She gave up teaching her Sabbath school class and pressed her hands over her ears when ringing bells called townsfolk to the services.

Lily eyed her warily but compressed her

lips and said nothing until one hot afternoon as they sat in the big rocking chairs on the wide veranda of Barbour Hall. "Emma, Dear, are you all right?" she began hesitantly. "You haven't been to prayer meeting with me in weeks."

"I'm tired," Emma snapped. Her face was set in tense lines and her eyes defied Lily to enter her thoughts.

"Feeding on God's Word rests and sustains me." Lily spoke gently.

Emma said nothing.

Lily sighed. Her soft, dark eyes were moist as she tried again. "Let me help. Have you and Jonathan quarreled?"

"No," Emma replied shortly. She opened the top button on the high neck of her white shirtwaist and fanned. "Well, not really." She looked at Lily, who leaned forward, eagerly trying to share her sorrow. Relenting slightly, she let out her breath and spoke in a wavering voice, "I'm beginning to think he won't ever be ready to — to marry . . ."

"It is a bad time," Lily replied quickly. Running her fingers through her dark hair, she said haltingly, "Try — to see his side of it. Don't shut him out. Share your thoughts." She sat for a moment looking down into the garden. "When I pray for Harrison, I am one with him across the

129

miles. Come with me tonight. You'll feel better if you'll let God . . ."

"No!" Emma flung out. Dry-eyed, her whole body drawn with misery, she clutched the arms of the rocker. "Why do you think God cares? The whole Confederacy is praying to Him. Maybe the Union is, too, but all we hear is report after report of bloody battles — death — disease!"

"Emmaaa!" Cordelia's coarse voice wailed from inside the house.

Jumping to her feet, glad for once to answer Cordelia's summons, Emma fled Lily without a backward glance.

The cold, wet wind that brought in November increased Cordelia's aguish neuralgia. Lily was dispatched to the drugstore to get more quinine.

Emma was in the upstairs hallway making certain that the round iron grate which conducted the summer heat up the grand staircase and out through the belvedere was now securely closed. Looking down on the landing below, she was surprised at the way Lily was dragging up the stairs.

"There is no more quinine," Lily said in hushed tones. Her face ashen, she bit her lip. "There will be no more."

Staring into Lily's frightened eyes, Emma gasped, "Whatever is the matter?"

CHAPTER 8

"They're evacuating the fort on Saint Vincent's." Lily's brown eyes were wide with alarm. "More vessels have been added to the blockade. Five schooners cleared the port in late November, but only one could get back in. The Federals have captured the rest and taken their loads of cotton and turpentine!"

"Jonathan?" Emma gasped, clutching her fists to her chest.

"No, no, he's all right. The *Hollycock* wasn't among them," Lily assured her. She sank to a chair and continued in a frightened voice. "I had a message from Harrison. They're withdrawing up the river."

Gurgling in Emma's throat bubbled out, half laughter, half tears.

"What will become of us," Cordelia Edwards wailed, "if the Yankees attack up the Chattahoochee?" She fell back, fanning rapidly.

As Lily turned to reassure her mother that many miles of fortified river still lay between them and the enemy, Emma went to the window and looked out through a blur of tears. Slowly a smile spread across her face and she lifted her shoulders. Jonathan could no longer run the dangerous blockade and risk being shut out of the country. Perhaps — probably — he was coming home.

Humming "Joy to the World," Emma hurried out to the kitchen to consult with Aunt Dilsey. "There will be no fruit for ambrosia. What can we have?" she queried.

Emma's high hopes and good spirits infected everyone. Happily, the servants speeded their pace, and Barbour Hall soon rang with laughter. The smell of Christmas filled every room.

Cheeks flushed, her hair escaping its knot into golden ringlets around her forehead, Emma was adding a final bit of holly to the central hall when a footstep on the veranda made her heart leap.

Turning joyfully with outstretched arms, she smiled into the dark and laughing eyes which had filled her dreams.

Bursting through the door without waiting for a formal invitation, Jonathan grasped her shoulders and beamed at her. "Oh,

Emma, dearest Emma, how I've missed you!"

They stood grinning foolishly, each renewing the joy of the other's face. Then he pushed her backward, making her blink in surprise. Shoving her beneath the crown-of-thorns chandelier, he crushed his lips upon hers. Blissfully, she returned his kiss, exalting because he had known without looking that she had covered the crystal teardrops with mistletoe.

Joy seasoned Christmas dinner. Ringing laughter filled the void left by unavailable delicacies. As if by unspoken rule, the war went unmentioned until all the traditions had been observed. Only after they had settled around the fireplace in the parlor did Jonathan break the drowsy silence.

"I have news I can't hold any longer," he exclaimed. "We've stopped running the blockade like so many puppies worrying an old cow. We're moving up-river to Saffold, and . . ."

"Aww," pouted Foy, disgusted that he had missed the sport.

"Why Saffold?" Cordelia Edwards roused from her dozing. "The Saffolds and David Johnston are old friends of my dear departed Mr. Edwards."

"It's on their plantation — not far from

that old mule-powered cotton gin — that the navy yard is building a gunboat."

"Where," Emma's voice squeaked. She cleared her throat and asked timidly, "Where is Saffold?"

"It's on the Georgia side of the river, down in Early County, less than a hundred miles from here."

Emma's eyes sparkled, and she drew in her breath delightedly as she beamed at Jonathan. A clear promise shone back from his eyes. With only a third as much of the river separating them as it had been to Apalachicola, they could often be together.

"We've merely tried to defend ourselves long enough," Jonathan spoke emphatically. "We're on the offensive now. Work was begun back in October on a gunboat named for the river, the *Chattahoochee*. I'll be at Saffold supervising completion, and training the crew, and . . ."

Extending his upturned hand toward Emma, he smiled at her tenderly. She could feel his warmth, and his yearning gesture told her that he, too, wished propriety allowed them more time alone.

"With a vessel such as this, we'll soon raise the blockade," he continued slowly, deliberately. His voice dropped and he leaned closer. "The war will soon be over and we can be married."

"How big is the gunboat?" Foy interrupted excitedly.

"Well," Jonathan turned. "She's a beauty. One hundred thirty feet long, thirty feet across at the beam, two engines to power two propellers —"

"What about you?" Lily turned worried eyes toward Harrison.

"Now that the river has risen, I'll be passing here constantly." He inclined his dark head toward hers and smiled reassuringly. "Florida's Governor Milton has ordered that no more cotton vessels be allowed to attempt leaving port because the Yankees are capturing too many prizes." He shrugged his shoulders expressively. "My work is reversed. Instead of taking cotton downriver to the sea, I'll just be going down as far as Saffold, loading bales from the plantation landings and taking them upriver to supply the cotton mills at Columbus. Uniforms, tents, and so on are being shipped out of there by rail."

Lily's brown curls bounced as she bobbed about the room. "And you'll be nearly empty going down, and we'll all —" Her voice rose to an excited squeal. "Oh, Mama, don't you want to visit Mrs. Johnston?"

Jonathan's spirit leaped across the

crowded room and locked with Emma's as vivacious Lily bubbled over with plans for them to visit Saffold. Emma sat with her head buzzing as dizzily as if he had actually whirled her in a waltz.

Even though the holidays were wet and cold, the family enjoyed pleasant, quiet hours by the fire. Embracing with smiles, Emma and Jonathan played backgammon or dominoes at the corner game table. In the adjoining library, Harrison helped Foy with trigonometry. Cordelia toasted her feet by the hearth and dictated the necessary letters to Lily to advise their friends of their upcoming visit. Since The Pines would be nearby, it was decided that they would also visit there.

"Oh, Emma!" Lily exclaimed. "You're going to love the Shackelford girls. They're delights."

"Real beauties, you say?" Jonathan perked up, feigning interest.

Emma merely smiled. Sustained by the loving warmth of Jonathan's presence, she wanted to savor each hour and not worry about the future.

They welcomed the New Year, 1862, buoyed by Jonathan's confidence that the Confederacy's new weapons would soon win the war. Eufaula celebrated and the band played "Home Again" as the *Chewalla* steamed into sight, bringing the Clayton Guards, the Pioneer Guards, and the Eufaula Rifles home after their twelve month's enlistment.

Jonathan and Harrison left with the promise that they would be reunited shortly; however, weather and circumstances created nerve-racking delays. Severe cold in January kept Cordelia in bed moaning with rheumatism. Terrifying thunderstorms shook February. Lightning struck a neighbor's house and raging fire consumed it.

The men came in March, bringing the dreadful news that the city of Apalachicola was in danger of falling. If the Confederates retreated, the Union raiders would begin pressing up the Apalachicola River, which flowed out of the Chattahoochee. The girls kept this news from Cordelia, Emma hoping steadfastly for their trip downriver. As yet the Yankees had not reached the Alabama line.

One morning when it seemed she could endure no more waiting, Emma walked into the garden and stretched her arms upward to a fresh-washed, watercolor sky. The trees, dressed in the yellow-green lace of young leaves, danced in the gentle breeze. In the distance, a low hum floated on the soft air. Gradually, the hollows of her loneliness began to fill until her very arms and legs reverberated with the sound of the steamboat's whistle.

Uhmmmmm! Uhmmmmm!

"Lily!" she screamed, running toward the house. "Lily!" she gasped, "The *Wave!*"

It looks like a floating wedding cake, Emma thought, smiling, nodding, and hugging herself as she approached the vessel, seeing it as if for the first time. The flat-bottomed boat, with its huge, side paddle wheel, rose in tiers of decks trimmed with white railings. Stained-glass windows sparkled like spun sugar in the hurricane deck. The tiny, airy pilothouse crowned the top. Emma laughed as she assisted Cordelia up the gangway. Normally, she was not fanciful; but then, she was usually going along as companion or chaperone. This trip was different. She was going to meet Jonathan.

Cordelia sniffed disdainfully as she hurried across the main deck just above the water's edge. Neither the cackling chickens nor the squealing pigs, waiting to be killed and served along the way, caused her to twist her nose. Rather, the frizzled and unwashed folk who crowded to the lower deck, ate the leftover grub stock, and scrambled ashore to help wood up the hungry engines twice each day, offended her sensibilities. Puffing, she climbed to the upper deck, where she settled back in a chair and prepared for a pleasant visit with friends.

Emma moved quietly through the group of broad-skirted, narrow-bonneted ladies and top-hatted gentlemen who crowded the deck so like a plantation gallery. The air tingled with anticipation as one huge paddle wheel reversed and the other turned forward. The tremendous boat backed smartly from the wharf and headed downriver. Lily and Mignonne were already established in the captain's stateroom. Emma need do nothing but lean against the rail, stare out at the green water shimmering in the sunshine, and dream of Jonathan and a home of her own.

The *Wave* floated gently, smoothly down the Chattahoochee, which was here smooth, there swirling swiftly over shoals, and always just ahead, turning through a green tunnel of trees shouldering their way to the water's edge. The crest of the high banks was guarded by ancient, dark green oaks. The bright red of infant maple leaves glistened along the slopes. Between them an impenetrable forest laced together with swags of vines blossoming with fragrant, yellow Jessamine. Emma leaned over the rail to look at the undulating green water. Wavering, she clutched her head.

"Dizzy?" asked Lily, joining her at the rail.

"Yes," admitted Emma ruefully. "I don't know why. There's no feeling of movement underfoot."

"Look straight ahead until you adjust," Lily advised. "It won't take long — oh, would you look at those sycamores stretching their arms out over the water. That white bark is so beautiful!"

Enchanted by the mystery of what lay beyond each turning, Lily leaned far out, pointing and admiring. Each time they reached a clearing, she waved vigorously to children running to see the steamboat pass and exclaimed that this imposing manor house was more beautiful than the last. Emma fretted because they stopped every few miles at yet another plantation landing to take on passengers, food, and cordwood for fuel. Would they never get to Saffold?

As the lazy day drifted to a close, they watched the colors of the sunset reflecting in the water over and again, rippling, sparkling, drifting, lifting. Relaxed, Emma suddenly realized that her dizziness was gone. Stretching and laughing, they got up from their deck chairs to dress for dinner.

Harrison and Lily presided over the festive meal. In the central hallway between the staterooms, long tables were set for fifty passengers. Chickens had been fricasseed; pigs had been roasted. Thick soups, heavily sauced Creole dishes, and platters of game were consumed by businessmen heading for the bustling river town of Columbia, Alabama; visiting ladies; and sundry other travelers. At the close of the meal, a rustle of ceremony claimed the attention of the diners. Two waiters carried in a tremendous birthday cake. Foy reddened with embarrassment and pleasure. At last he was sixteen.

The Italian orchestra was no longer traveling with the *Wave* because of the war; however, the congenial group went into the ladies' saloon, and Emma obliged by playing waltzes on the Chickering grand piano.

Excitement pounded in Emma's temples as they completed their unloading and pulled away from Columbia at last. The scenery began to change. Limestone outcroppings made the river more dangerous with hidden shallows. The hardwood trees gave way to towering, black-green pines. Their spring growth made them look as if their branches were set with golden candles.

When at last they reached their destination and prepared to leave the steamer, Foy grinned at Emma. "I wish we could go straight to the navy yard," he whispered.

"Me, too," she replied, "but we'll have to be patient a little longer."

The family climbed into the carriage which had been sent to meet them, and rode a short distance through piney woods, before the sandy road suddenly turned.

"Oh!" Lily drew in her breath in delight. "Oh, I'd forgotten how beautiful the live oaks are." She sighed as they drove down the long, cool avenue.

Dressed in the glistening, dark green velvet of tiny evergreen leaves, hoop-skirted trees lifted their arms and intertwined their fingers over the roadway. Each spreading arm and dipping elbow was draped with gray lace shawls of Spanish moss. "They look like ladies-in-waiting for a bridal procession," Lily declared.

Emma blushed but said nothing.

"These coastal live oaks are one of the main reasons that the shipyard is here at Saffold," Harrison said. "Their strong, yellow wood is very durable underwater."

"Surely they won't cut these!" Lily drew up indignantly.

"Well, not the *allée* to the house, I'm

sure," he laughed.

At the end of the lane, the Johnston home glistened whitely. Lofty, round columns of heart pine marched across the spreading portico where Mrs. Johnston graciously welcomed them.

By midafternoon Emma was nervously fidgeting, wondering how she could ever politely ask to see the gunboat.

Mrs. Johnston looked up at her with her plump face wreathed in understanding smiles. "We're all invited to a little tea aboard the *Chattahoochee* this afternoon, my dear. We frequently entertain the officers and the young ladies of the neighborhood; consequently, they are returning our hospitality."

Stiff with disappointment because of her failure to spot Jonathan as the party went up the gangway to the *Chattahoochee,* Emma followed the group about. Awestruck, she threw back her head and looked straight upward at the three towering masts of the 130-foot vessel. The first lieutenant conducting their tour explained that while the masts would be sail rigged, the light-draft vessel was also steam-driven by a double propeller.

Misery overwhelmed her and she could scarcely feign attention as they watched workmen mounting the battery, which would consist of four broadside cannon, and forward and aft pivot guns. She gave up trying to look wise and hurried below to the officers' quarters. Surely Jonathan would be there arranging the tea.

Surprisingly, flowers in great profusion filled the wardroom. Three exquisitely gowned young ladies were introduced to her as some of the Shackelford girls who had come down from The Pines. Their mother had sent the flowers, a great market basket of strawberries, some cream, and a pound cake. She murmured small talk as she nibbled the rich dessert, but her eyes kept straying to the doors of the officers' cabins on both sides. Her mind struggled to decide if she had misunderstood. Jonathan *was* stationed aboard the *Chattahoochee,* wasn't he?

The hair on the back of Emma's neck prickled and the space between her shoulders burned. Turning quickly, she saw him as he climbed down from the gun deck. Laughing, shaking hands, he made slow progress across the crowded wardroom, but his twinkling eyes were upon her.

Glowing, Emma stood waiting. At last, he reached her and bowed formally, kissing her hand.

"Miss Edwards, how lovely you look in my favorite pink." His charming smile became a boyish grin as he whispered, "Emma, Dearest, how I've missed you!"

"I was beginning to think I'd misunderstood," she answered softly.

"I'm sorry I wasn't here to meet you," he apologized. "I've only just arrived from the Naval Ironworks at Columbus. I was ordered to bring down a raft loaded with machinery and cannon." He squeezed her hand and jerked his head in the direction of the door, but he continued speaking formally. "We have some very valuable weapons. Have you seen the Dahlgren?"

Happily, she followed him up to the gun deck and stood looking at the dark curl which fell over his forehead as he excitedly showed her the shiny pivot-mounted gun.

"There's none better for naval action," he exclaimed enthusiastically. "The *Chattahoochee* is a first-class gunboat. Even unfinished, she could hold off the Yankees." He led her along the deck of the square-rigged schooner, and she wondered if she were about to receive another tour. When they reached the secluded shadow of the towering smokestack, he leaned close above her and whispered. "Darling Emma, this war will soon be over. With these new weapons, we'll lick the enemy. Then I can give myself completely to you!"

She could only whisper, "I love you."

Jonathan gazed down at her with an intensity which reddened her cheeks and made her shiver like a puppy. He kissed her with heightened urgency. His voice husky with emotion, he promised, "Soon, we'll be man and wife!"

Standing at the rail with her golden head as close to his dark curls as they dared without raising everyone's eyebrows, they discussed wedding arrangements and whispered endearments. All too soon the group was spilling around them, babbling excited plans for the evening. Incredulous that the way was prepared for them to be together, they learned that the officers and ladies were all invited to visit The Pines.

The Shackelford plantation covered three thousand acres, many miles of which stretched along the Chattahoochee. From the moment they approached the house and saw candles twinkling from every window upstairs and down, and laughing couples drifting in and out through French doors onto the wide piazza, Emma sensed a welcoming atmosphere, a quiet peace far removed from the ugliness of war.

Even though Jonathan and his fellow officers wore uniforms resplendent with gold braid and brass buttons, they faded into insignificance beside the exquisite gowns of the ladies. While some of the men wore Confederate gray, others were attired in dark blue flannel. These officers formerly had been in the United States Navy, and they preferred to continue to wear the color they deemed universal for men of the sea.

Jonathan had just introduced Emma to his friend, Cowles Myles Collier, when the handsome, former West Point cadet's attention became riveted upon the curving staircase. Two beautiful girls, identically gowned in apricot silk, matching the highlights of their spiraling auburn curls, floated down. Identical smiles puzzled onlookers as to which twin was Hannah and which was Georgie. When Collier hurried to bow before one of them, Jonathan whispered, "That must be Hannah."

A beautiful girl with a crown of brown curls drifted down the stairs with a quiet elegance, to be identified by Jonathan as Ellen. Emma quickly searched his face for signs that he might be interested in this quietly restrained girl.

Some of the older Shackelford girls and their husbands also joined the group which assembled in the dining room, a seeming

147

fairyland of white and gold. Massive arrangements of white iris and sprays of bridal wreath spirea were reflected in the gleaming mahogany sideboard. Their delicate perfume filled the room. The long table was covered with snowy white linen and set with gold-banded white china. Candlelight gleamed on the silver, twinkled in the crystal, and sparkled in Emma's eyes as she basked in Jonathan's full attention.

Supper was bountiful. Emma noticed only a slight flat taste from the scarcity of salt and lack of foreign spices. The food was delightfully aromatic with herbs from the kitchen garden. Because the plantation raised most of the food, the fare did not look as meager as their table in town where the supply in the stores had become alarmingly short. Pleasant conversation flowed as they remained long at the table eating course after course.

When at last they moved into the parlor, Hannah and Georgie captivated the party by singing duets, accompanied by Ellen on the piano. Then, as the group separated into playing chess, writing letters home from well-supplied desks, reading books by oil lamps, or talking with their host, James Shackelford, in his invalid's chair. Jonathan grasped Emma's elbow and guided her

148

quietly through a French door to the piazza. Saying nothing as they moved along the wide veranda, Emma could feel her face glowing in the moonlight. She touched her fingers to her cheeks and sighed rapturously.

"All through the meal I dreamed of the time when you'll be hostess at our table at Magnolia Springs." Jonathan smiled down at her, holding her hands tightly. "But —" He arched his black brows and asked anxiously, "After being accustomed to a cosmopolitan place like Eufaula, can you be happy on an isolated plantation?" Then he added quickly, "If you wanted to visit a city, we're not far from Savannah."

"I can be happy anywhere as long as it's with you," she breathed. The tightness in Emma's chest from her long-stored love was released in a flood of happiness. "I'd adore plantation living. The easy pace, the quiet simplicity . . ."

Satisfied, Jonathan drew her into the shadows and slipped his arm around her shoulders to shield her from the chill night air. Time was softly suspended. It seemed only moments before the servants appeared to signal family prayers.

Then the guests were shown to their rooms where high feather beds were turned down and servants stood smiling, ready to supply every need.

Emma wanted to relive each lovely moment, but she drifted into peaceful slumber only to be awakened by neighing and whinnying. Looking out of her window, she saw horses being brought to the block. Jonathan was among the early risers joining Ellen Shackelford and a group of riders for a brisk canter along the bridle paths of The Pines.

Smiling, stretching, enjoying the luxury of not being at the beck and call of Cordelia, who had remained with Mrs. Johnston, Emma leisurely completed her toilette. She chose a white dimity sprigged with delicate sprays of pastel flowers. Nodding at her reflection in the looking glass, she confirmed that this simple, fitted bodice, with the detailing on the sleeves from elbow to wrist and lace falling around her expressive hands, suited her and the occasion better than a multitude of ruffles. She brushed her hair and let it fall loosely. There was no use trying to contain it in the March breeze.

At midmorning, the party climbed into carriages and buggies. Followed by a wagon loaded with picnic hampers, they drove through woods of slender, sharp-scented pines along roads of deep, shifting sand. Sharp bayonets of palmetto, crowding beneath the tall evergreens, threatened the dainty dogwoods' snowy lace.

Soon after they turned south from the River Road toward Glenn Springs, the overpowering smell of rotten eggs made Emma want to hold her breath. Her wry face provoked much laughter as the group reached the picnic area by a spring which bubbled out of lime rock. Finally, they persuaded her that it was the healthful thing to do to drink sulfur water, especially in the springtime. She turned down her mouth and shuddered. The water tasted fully as bad as it smelled.

Setting up an easel, Myles Collier began to paint the elfin Hannah as she posed by the spring. Ellen sat on a stump and strummed her guitar and sang "My Nannie O." Sitting about on quilts, the group joined dreamily in singing Stephen Foster's "Jeanie with the Light Brown Hair."

Floating on the melody, Jonathan and Emma strolled the woodland on a brown, pine-needle carpet. Meandering hand in hand, smiling softly at each other, they wandered beneath the whispering pines high above them in the restless wind and listened to the endless tunes of the mockingbirds. The dogwoods, completely covered with white blossoms, made Emma think of brides and bridesmaids. Filled with longing, she wanted to tell Jonathan that she had changed her mind about preferring to be married in Eufaula. Nowhere could be lovelier than Saffold just now, and she felt certain that the motherly Mrs. Johnston would be delighted to give her a wedding.

Looking up at Jonathan, she failed to watch where she was going. Piercing swords of palmetto stabbed her drifting dimity skirt, halting her progress until Jonathan cut her free with a pocketknife. As she sat down on a mossy log to work the prickly pieces loose from the sheer material, Jonathan cut a branch of dogwood over her head and sat down beside her.

"Dogwood always makes me think of the Resurrection," he said. "The petals form a cross, with the rusty notches of the nail prints in the tips and the crown of thorns in the center."

Soberly Emma took the flowers he offered. This was Jonathan different from his laughing, joking self. Sensing that it was not the time to rush him about a wedding, she was content as they talked of their thoughts and feelings and got to know each other more fully. With his arm around her shoulders and his head so close to hers, she joyfully discovered what Lily had meant by being one with a man in mind and spirit.

Tenderly, lovingly, he kissed her before they rejoined the other couples for a gay picnic by the spring.

Suddenly, a damp, chill wind snatched at the tablecloth. They had not noticed a black cloud rolling in. Large, cold raindrops pelted them as they scurried about, packing, running, hitching the horses, jumping into the carriages, becoming thoroughly soaked by the time they reached The Pines.

Young Horry Dent was there with a summons for Jonathan. Standing waiting for him in the hallway, Emma frowned at her bedraggled skirt as she noticed for the first time the spot of blood where she had cut her finger on the palmetto. When Jonathan came at last to her side, his eyes were glittering. His relaxed posture had suddenly become stiffly, militarily erect.

"I must return to duty at once," he said briskly. "Horry Dent has been transferred here as assistant engineer. He just came down from Columbus on a raft loaded with hardware, and he brought tremendous news!"

To Emma his eyes seemed suddenly as hard and impenetrable as his brass buttons. She could no longer follow his thoughts. "What news?" she asked meekly.

"Everything has changed." He swallowed

excitedly. "The whole of naval warfare has been revolutionized!" He sprang from one foot to the other, eager to leave. "Catesby Jones is coming to take command of the *Chattahoochee.* Things will start to pop." He nodded his head. "It won't be long, Emma. We'll be married just as soon as the South wins the war!"

CHAPTER 9

"Catesby Jones? Who is he? How can one man — make such a difference?" Emma stammered. "How can everything change so quickly?" The excitement in Jonathan's voice had carried around the entrance hall. The men pressed closer. The ladies paused, draped along the staircase, dabbing at dripping curls.

With all eyes upon him, Jonathan explained. "Jones is a hero of one of our greater Confederate victories! It will be handed down in history as one of the prime achievements of this war," he declared in ringing tones. "The first battle between ships of iron!"

"Iron?"

"Iron ships?"

Curiosity buzzed through the group. Some of the girls shrugged and continued up the stairs to change their rain-soaked frocks, but Emma remained. Clinging to the banister, she strained to see Jonathan's face. A sickened feeling that this news held portent for her life with him made her clutch her hands together as he shared news he had received.

"As you all know, when the United States Navy left the Grosport Navy Yard across from Norfolk when Virginia seceded, they didn't have time to take all their vessels so they set some afire. There was one, the USS *Merrimack,* which burned to the waterline and sank." His dark eyes were gleaming with excitement. "Our men have raised her hull, cut off the sides, and covered what was left with iron plates. They renamed their armored warship the CSS *Virginia.*"

Emma plucked at the wet dimity clinging to her throat and held her breath. Jonathan had completely forgotten her presence.

"Can't you just imagine what she looked like?" He gestured wildly. "The five Yankee vessels dozing in the harbor at Hampton Roads must have thought a giant turtle had risen from the sea sprouting guns. The *Cumberland* opened fire; but the shells bounced off that hard shell, and the *Virginia* — or *Merrimack,* if you please — took one snap at the *Cumberland*'s wooden sides and sank her, then burned the *Congress* with red-hot shot from her guns."

A cheer resounded through the entry hall.

"Lieutenant Jones was the executive officer — wait . . ." Jonathan held up his hand to stifle another cheer. "There's more. The next morning when they returned to finish the job, an iron raft came out to meet them, the Federals' ironclad, the *Monitor*. She was only a quarter the size of the *Virginia* with only one gun set in the center like a big, round cheesebox, but . . . ," he paused for effect, "it revolved — making it a hopeless target."

"The battle lasted four hours," Horry Dent piped up from the doorway, unable to control his excitement. "Thousands of people stood on the shore cheering them on."

"When Admiral Buchanan was severely wounded, Jones became commander and dueled the *Monitor*," Jonathan continued. "They finally withdrew. Neither could do much harm to the other's iron sides."

"All the old navies of the world will be useless," shouted Myles Collier above the ensuing clamor. "We'll have to discard wooden vessels and build ironclads —" He started for the door as if ready to begin, then stopped short, "What will this mean for the future of the *Chattahoochee*?"

"I don't know," replied Jonathan. "But

plans for building an ironclad based on the *Virginia* are being made at Columbus. With such a ram we can easily cut through the blockade . . ."

The men were leaving, walking out into a reverberating thunderstorm, as oblivious to the lion's roar of the March wind as to the anxious, longing looks of the ladies.

War had scraped its horrid finger against the surface of their placid haven. Everything changed. No longer was it difficult to differentiate between the twins. Hannah was in constant tears. Myles Collier had asked for her hand in marriage before he shipped out, but her father refused permission. Even though Collier was from one of the first families of Virginia, James Shackelford had a deep-seated prejudice against soldiers and sailors. Lily sympathized with Hannah, recalling her own dilemma when her parents refused to let her marry Harrison. Emma, however, had difficulty swallowing bitterness. No one had refused her permission to wed — except the groom.

Stony-faced, refusing to give way to tears, Emma packed her trunk. Even if they could have imposed longer upon their hosts, Jonathan had no time for her. He was totally occupied with drilling the seventy-eight men required to man the guns of the *Chatta-*

hoochee. Since the vessel was so nearly finished, it was decided to complete her before putting all efforts into constructing the ironclad with the yard name *Muscogee.*

With their lovely idyll ended, Emma rode back through the avenue of live oaks, head down. She could not bear to look at their graceful ladies-in-waiting. Reverberating cannon blasts assaulted her ears when they reached the wharf. Jonathan was so intent upon the target practice that he did not notice her when she climbed the gangway to the *Wave.*

Uhmmmmm! Uhmmmmm!

At the departing signal Jonathan turned, threw his hand high and smiled across the water.

Emma wanted to throw herself upon her bunk in a fit of weeping, but she had to stand over the prostrate Cordelia. If Jonathan had asked her to remain behind as a bride, it would have been difficult to tear herself from her sister-in-law. Cordelia was inconsolable because Foy was not returning to Eufaula with them. Sixteen now, suddenly tall, looking like a walking broomstick, he joined the crew of the *Chattahoochee.*

The women arrived in an almost-deserted Eufaula. The men of the Clayton Guards had plowed their lands for spring planting,

159

but with the acceleration of the war they returned to service. The Eufaula Rifles had disbanded. Now, the Eufaula Light Artillery was organized and moved out on March 26. Two days later the older men of the town organized the Minutemen to provide the women and children some protection.

Prowling the house each night, Emma bolted doors. Barbour Hall echoed hollowly without the constant antics of Foy and his friends, now all enlisted in the army or navy. Emma moved woodenly through her nursing chores with a loneliness that enveloped her soul. Jonathan's preoccupation with mounting an offensive seemed to have shut her out.

The frightening report came that Apalachicola had been evacuated on March 14, Emma's twenty-ninth birthday. Groups of women and children had snatched up what they could on short notice, leaving in a deluge of cold rain. The rising river threatened to carry them away, but they reached a low bluff upriver and lay in the mud until late the next day when rafts and flats arrived to take them over the flooded countryside.

Nervously, Emma and Lily joined the throng in town awaiting news. Finally they heard that on April 3, Commander H. S.

Stellwagen had landed the *Mercedia* at Apalachicola and demanded the remaining secessionists surrender. The Confederate troops had withdrawn fifty-seven miles upriver to fortify Ricko's Bluff. In April, the steamer *Jackson* somehow made it through the blockade. When it passed Eufaula headed for Columbus with a load of ten thousand rifles for the Confederacy, Emma sank into silence with sickening certainty that the war would not soon be over but had settled down to a long and bloody siege.

One sunny morning in mid-May Lily arrived, as effervescent as usual, with Mignonne talking excitedly about the birds' nest her mother had showed her. Lily's brown eyes sparkled as she waited for her daughter to finish her tale before speaking excitedly, "The *Wave* is headed for Saffold. Do you feel like going, Mama?"

"No, no, I don't feel like it," sighed Cordelia, pale against the pillows of her massive bed. "But," she rose heavily, unplaiting her hair, "if I'm to see Foy, I must."

Emma began to breathe again.

Everything in Saffold had changed — no tea parties. Formerly flirting seamen now moved purposefully about assigned tasks. Emma eyed each uniformed back, but she did not see Jonathan. Although she almost felt his beloved boat was her rival, she laughed at herself and admitted the freshly painted *Chattahoochee* was beautiful with her slender, stone-colored hull and sails now swelling in the breeze.

Even Cordelia went on a tour of the gunboat this time. Following Foy, she negotiated her hoop skirt down the ladder into the crew's quarters with difficulty. Grinning until his ears seemed to flap, Foy showed them the berth deck and pointed out his hammock, a canvas only two feet wide fastened at the ends, onto hooks driven into the deck beams.

"They knew I was green, and they strung up my hammock as tightly as they could." Foy laughed. "I climbed in and tumbled right out. All that first night either I or the mattress was falling out, but I learned to bag it in the middle so the sides turn up. Now, I have no trouble sleeping in my dream bag — except getting enough time in it."

Cordelia declined going down in the hold area, but she did take a quick look at the engine room with its huge boilers. Lagging behind, Emma drew back from the menacing sound of hissing steam.

"Don't worry," Foy calmed them. Proud of his knowledge, he explained, "We're waiting for more iron to close a hole in the smokestack before we can get up sufficient steam to turn the two propellers."

Trailing Cordelia about the gun deck, Emma kept glancing around in hopes of seeing Jonathan. Idly she asked Foy why the boxes of sand had been placed there.

"Oh, that's so we won't slip on the blood on deck during a battle," he said casually.

Cordelia gasped. Emma paled. What had happened to the assurances of bloodless war?

Turning, Emma saw Jonathan at last. He was striding across the deck to greet her. "Catesby Jones hasn't arrived," he said without even asking how she was. "We can't seem to get the *Chattahoochee* completed and ready for action." He spoke agitatedly as he moved back and forth between Emma and a workman fitting a rifled cannon. "We must get on the offensive! But we can't secure the iron to complete the engines, and we're running out of time!"

Emma murmured noncommittally. She saw that he had no room left in his thoughts for loving words.

"All plans are at variance," he complained to her. Distraught, he raked his fingers through his black curls. "The small garrison on Ricko's Bluff has a battery of only ten guns." He shook his head. "Pitifully inadequate protection for an area where eighty thousand bales of cotton were stored. Many of our officials are calling for obstructions to be sunk in the river to block the Federals' sailing upstream."

Emma looked at him with her blue eyes wide, questioning. She did not grasp his meaning; but the frantic note in his voice indicated that he did not know which way to turn, and she longed to comfort him.

"Don't you see? When the *Chattahoochee* and *Muscogee* are completed, we must be able to get downstream if we are ever to attack and break the blockade!"

The heated argument among the Confederate officials about whether or not to stop passage on the river by filling it with impassable objects was not settled by the time the *Wave* was loaded. Their party had to board the steamboat without knowing what was to be done.

By the time the whistle signaled departure, people had arrived from all directions and crowded onto the decks of the *Wave,* many of them refugees from Pensacola or Apalachicola, drawn together by the sudden realization of the horrors of war. Bit by more terrible bit of the bloody battles as the Federal Army tried to take the Confederate capital Richmond, Virginia, had filtered in.

One young woman, attired in black taffeta and heavy mourning veils, fainted from the intense heat, unusual for early June. Making her way through the crush of passengers, Emma reached the woman's side with a basin of water. As she pushed back the veil and bathed the ashy face, the woman spoke.

"My name is Mary Allison," she said. "I've been riding all day through the pine woods to get here. I know all of the staterooms are occupied, and I shall have to sit up all night; but, oh, I just must try to claim my husband's body." A sob wracked her. "We've been married a year, but we only spent one month together. Oh, this is a hard, cruel war!"

Emma knelt beside Mary and watched helplessly as uncontrollable weeping overwhelmed her. Around them flowed anguished stories of relatives going to Richmond to visit wounded brothers or husbands. The whole town of Marianna, Florida, was in mourning since the news had come of the appalling slaughters on May 31 and June 1, south of Richmond at Seven Pines and Chickahominy.

A country doctor, who confessed he had never extracted a bullet or dressed a fractured limb but was going to offer his services to the army, knelt beside Emma and took Mary's hands.

Noise and confusion reigned until at last Harrison arranged for the gentlemen to rest as best they could in the saloon and the ladies to appropriate all the berths.

Emma lay awake far into the night thinking of poor Mary Allison. Jonathan would say they should not have married. But they had had one month to remember. Hot tears soaked her pillow before she slept.

The next morning the ladies waited amiably to make their toilettes as the stewardess passed from one room to the other with the only handbasin left on board. Once the *Wave* had been famous for the elegance of her fittings; those who knew this were able to shrug off the inconvenience.

The sun had risen, a ball of heat. Seeking relief on the shady side of the boat, Emma found that Lily had made friends with an Englishwoman who had been governess to Florida Governor Milton's children. Frightened by the war news, Sarah Jones had been unable to leave through the blockaded Gulf ports; consequently, she was heading north in hopes of escaping to England through Richmond. Lily and Sarah Jones were drawn together by their love of nature. They stood at the rail admiring the luxuriant foliage on the banks. Emma looked at the blood-red blossoms of vines which strangled some of the tallest pines and could not share their enthusiasm. She had never been in such a crowd, yet felt so alone.

The seemingly interminable trip dragged on with stops at nearly every plantation landing. "Great cotton speculations are going on," Lily explained to the foreign visitor. "The planters are hurrying to ship the cotton to the interior where it is being bought up by speculators for fifteen cents a pound."

"Oh, but it's wasting," cried Miss Jones, gesturing up the rugged precipice as cotton bales slid down a wooden chute to the river.

Feeling dazed by the hot, west wind burning her cheeks, Emma silently looked up the cliff where Miss Jones pointed. Giddily she felt that she, too, was poised on a precipice about to plunge.

"Why build six-story warehouses way up there?" the Englishwoman demanded indignantly, her face florid beneath carroty hair. She ran along the deck where a bale, with casing torn and cords broken, was spreading apart, whitening the muddy stream. "Oh," she cried again, "my countrymen in Liverpool and Lancashire are starving in penury, out of work without cotton. Oh, the unattainable path of cotton on Rebel waters, floating away on the windings of the river!" Miss Jones turned back angrily to face them. "Has no one ambition to build at the water level?"

Patiently, Lily pointed to the water marks on the warehouses and trees sixty feet above their heads. "The Chattahoochee has sudden and excessive rises by season," she explained. "In summer the bridge at Eufaula is eighty feet above the river, but once the water was so high a steamboat passed round the side of the bridge over the cotton fields."

Emma felt little patience with Sarah Jones as she complained over dinner that the Southern heat was making her ill and the very plate and fork were burning her hand. Emma laughed to herself at the stocky, robust girl and paid little attention as she expounded at length on how the war should be settled. Emma's blue eyes glazed as she let her mind drift to Jonathan. Suddenly she blinked and focused, aware that Sarah Jones was addressing her directly.

"Why do you make obeisance to that domineering Edwards woman?" she snapped. "Are you her servant?"

"Um, well, no, uh," Emma stammered,

shocked.

"Emma's my aunt," Lily interjected quickly, her liquid eyes not leaving Emma's hurt face. "In our realm of society, one lives with the nearest relative if — if . . ."

"If you're unfortunate enough to be a 'maiden lady'," Emma finished bitterly.

"Why don't you get a job?" Miss Jones puffed herself to her full five feet. "You should do as I do. I've been a governess all over your country." If she had made the connection between Lily and Mrs. Edwards, she was not embarrassed. She stared at them haughtily as they both opened their mouths but said nothing.

"Well, you see," Lily faltered, "there's just no job acceptable to a lady — here — and . . . ," she finished brightly, "Emma's engaged to be married." Lily smiled sweetly and lifted Emma's rubied hand.

"We're just waiting for the war to be over." Emma's voice was flat and her face felt too pinched to smile.

"Humph! You're mighty old to start a family," Miss Jones retorted.

"Not really. I long for children," she answered softly.

"I teach children." The governess tossed her carroty hair.

"I used to teach at Sabbath school," said

Emma, wondering why she kept replying. Wincing, she realized that she had given up the pleasure of being with the children when she stopped attending church because she felt God did not care.

With the meal over at last, Emma withdrew further and further into a shell of silence. By Sunday afternoon when they scrambled up the steep bank at Eufaula, with Sarah grumbling about the idle men's failure to build steps, Emma felt incapable of words.

Looking up, she saw Kitty and Lige grinning at her, crossing the bridge to Georgetown, Georgia. She knew they frequently took the train to Americus to attend the church where they had been baptized, and she merely nodded to them in her misery.

The servants, however, were bent upon attracting their attention; she mustered the energy to compliment Kitty who was dressed in a new crinoline-stiffened skirt of the latest western style but had wrapped her head in a turban of the East. Resplendent in heavy gold rings and neck chains, Lige stood holding Kitty's fan and parasol. Emma admired his fancy cravat, and he smiled broadly so that his gold tooth sparkled in the sunlight.

They seemed to know so little of the

bloodshed. Emma tried to smooth the frown from her face and not spoil their carefree gaiety. Sticky-hot, dirty, feeling tired and very old, she could not manage a smile.

Riding through Eufaula on the way to Barbour Hall, Emma sighed over the melancholy effects of the war and the blockade. She realized how forlorn their proud town must look to Sarah Jones. Jagged glass turned the drugstore window into an evil grin, the few remaining bottles looking like scattered teeth. Boards closed most of the shops. The *clopping* of their horse's hooves resounded in deserted streets, peopled only by the hotel guests. Could Lily's prayers and Jonathan's new weapons save them?

The echoing emptiness of the marble floors of Barbour Hall seemed to mimic the hollowness of Emma's heart. It seemed scarcely to beat until news came that the *Wave* had been summoned to return to Saffold.

CHAPTER 10

"My beautiful *Wave,* a warship," wailed Lily. Throwing back her head, she clung to the rail and looked above her at the hurricane deck where once the orchestra had played. She wiped tears and spoke in a strained voice. "Oh, Harrison! How different times are now than when we danced in the moonlight on the decks of this boat of dreams. Will we ever again have beauty and peace and loving our neighbor?"

Harrison's arm enclosed her in a safe little world of their own. "One day." He smiled down at her with tender understanding. "*Ma chére,* one day our world shall sing again." He stroked his hand along the ship's rail. "I love her, too, but she must be armed to protect our home and our pretty Mignonne."

Standing on the deck with Harrison and Lily, yet terribly, unbearably alone, Emma thought bitterly that the *Wave* was part of their oneness. The *Chattahoochee* seemed a rival, a wedge between her and Jonathan. Glancing at them out of the corner of her eye, she watched their rapt expressions. Emma's longing for this kind of love, love that had grown deeper with time, was more painful than when she had stood in the shadows playing the part of their chaperone. Then, she had had no hope of a life of her own. She had shut up her heart and moved through her days doing what was required of her. Now, since she had opened her heart to Jonathan, fear that he might not really love or marry her tore at the ragged, bleeding edges.

Arriving at the Saffold Navy Yard, they stepped into a scene of intense activity. The muscles in Emma's legs ached with tension as she followed the Wingates up the gangway on the *Chattahoochee.* A smile quivered on her cheeks, and she stood openmouthed as Jonathan came striding purposefully across the deck to meet them. How alive he looked, how handsome — with his feet stepping quickly to the rhythm of the wind in the rigging, and his eyes dancing with excitement. Her yearning heart reached out to him, but he greeted them hurriedly. His smile brushed over her, and he turned and gestured.

"May I present Captain Catesby Jones," Jonathan said enthusiastically. "Now that he's taken command, we'll clear our river of the enemy for sure!"

Captain Jones bowed graciously over their hands. He moved with military bearing and self-assurance, but he rubbed his hand over his balding head and spoke self-deprecatingly. "We'll do our best, but we're frustrated at the delays in finishing the boilers because of the lack of iron. The Union is building with iron by the ton while we receive fifty pounds at a time, melted down from church bells and other cherished objects."

Emma stood trembling, trying to listen to the men's brisk discussion of their problems. Coherent thoughts were blocked by her longing to reach out and touch Jonathan's cheek, gone slack with inadequacy, to brush the dark curl from eyes now filled with worry. Suddenly Jones gave some command. Jonathan bowed over her hand and was gone.

Disappointed, hurt, she rode unseeingly up the avenue of live oaks. Somehow, in spite of the shortages, the amazing Mrs. Johnston continued to entertain them all graciously, planning that evening's dinner party to include the officers of the gunboat.

Emma dressed with shaking hands, then sat nervously in a corner of the parlor. She half-rose at the sound of Jonathan's voice in the foyer, but two local girls rushed to his side, coquettishly fanning and flirting. They chattered incessantly about riding with him down the river on an expedition to lay torpedoes.

Stinging with jealousy, Emma gritted her teeth. How could she convey to them that her ruby necklace and ring were engagement gifts from Jonathan Ramsey? Sulkily, she sat waiting for him to cross the room to her. It seemed forever before he disengaged himself from the local belles. She picked up a stereoscope and pretended to be interested in the photographs.

"Darling Emma." Jonathan smiled down at her. "Time begins again now that you are here!" He squeezed her hand as he bowed over it and kissed it, then held it lovingly to his cheek.

Blood rushed to her face, and she drew the first relaxed breath she had had in weeks. "Oh, Jonathan," she whispered, "time doesn't move at all when I'm away from you." She nodded eager assent to the jerk of his head and stood quickly to follow him into the sanctuary of the garden. Before they reached the French door onto the piazza, a commotion in the entrance hall stopped them.

An arrogantly handsome young man in a sharply pressed, dark blue flannel uniform entered the parlor, immediately focusing the attention of everyone in the room upon him. Emma's lovely moment shattered at her feet. With her hand at her constricted throat, she saw the glitter of excitement in Jonathan's eyes as he turned back to be introduced.

"Beg pardon a moment." Jonathan nodded absently to her. "We've been awaiting Lieutenant George Gift. He's fresh from a brilliant and successful engagement of the sloop of war *Arkansas* in the battles on the Mississippi near Vicksburg. She's an ironclad ram such as the *Muscogee* will be." He left her side and joined the men gathered around Gift to hear his tales of action they eagerly awaited.

Dejected, yet trying to maintain a smile, Emma blotted out the bloody details until she heard him say the *Arkansas* had blown up and he had escaped by swimming. With his story ended, Gift's eyes lighted on Ellen Shackelford, seated at the far end of the parlor. Waving his hand at the men to indicate that they had talked enough of battle, he strode across the room to Ellen's side and bowed before her.

Only then did Jonathan and Emma step out into the garden. As they strolled paths sharply scented with boxwood, he continued to talk of war. He explained that Captain Jones and Gift, his first lieutenant, were Annapolis graduates who had served together in the U.S. Navy.

Her emotions as tremulous as the moonlight, she merely nodded, afraid to speak. Fighting tears, she lifted her chin defiantly and tried to steel herself. She had gotten along alone all these years. She could do it again. She needed no one, nothing. Clearly, this man was too enthralled with the war to need her as she longed for — no, she would not give way. She straightened her drooping shoulders and concentrated on his voice, which was pitched high with enthusiasm.

"With two officers so experienced in battle, we shall soon engage the enemy and break their blockade. Then, Emma —" He took both her hands and dropped a gentle kiss on the golden tendrils on her forehead. "Then, my darling Emma," his voice became a hoarse whisper, "our time will come at last."

In the peaceful beauty of the garden, paths beckoned in all directions. Guiding her behind the dense screen of a magnolia,

Jonathan suddenly swept her into his arms. Hungrily he kissed her. Responding with all her pent-up longing, Emma twined her arms about his neck, knotted her fingers in his springy, black curls, and returned his kiss joyfully. Breathlessly, she pushed back at last and laughed softly.

He did not release her. Keeping his arms tightly around her, he kissed her eyes, her hair, as she gasped for breath. "Emma, dearest, dearest Emma," he whispered against her ear, kissed it, laughed as she shivered. "Soon, soon we will be married!"

Doubts and fears forgotten, Emma lifted her shining face to his. Unable to speak through her flooding happiness, she tiptoed and answered him with a kiss.

Approaching footsteps and murmuring voices told them that other couples were joining them in the garden. Discreetly, they pulled apart to stroll contentedly hand in hand through the moonlit garden, unnoticing of fall's nip in the air. Late roses wafted intoxicating perfume around their happy faces. Needing no communication save the touching of hands, they said little. Suddenly they realized that the garden had become quiet. The moon had scudded across the sky; the lovely evening was over. Tenderly, Jonathan lifted her chin, smiled, kissed her.

They reluctantly crossed the piazza and rejoined the other couples in the parlor.

George Gift's animation gave evidence of the fact he was completely smitten with the dainty Ellen. As the guests departed, Gift and Jones conferred briefly. The captain rubbed his hand over his balding head, pulled his beard, then smiled.

The dashing Gift turned, bowed gallantly, and said, "Ladies, we would like to invite you to join us tomorrow for an entertainment aboard the *Chattahoochee!*"

Cheering went up from the men in the rigging as the ladies' carriages arrived at the riverside. Fluttering banners welcomed them with the stars and bars of the Confederacy flying at each masthead and the colorful Spanish, French, and English flags at the end of the gaff.

Beaming, Jonathan took Emma's pink parasol and squeezed the ruby on her finger as he helped her aboard. Standing beside him, she relaxed happily and enjoyed the crisp breeze on her face as the *Chattahoochee* floated down her namesake. No one mentioned the fact that she had to be towed by a small steamer because her own engines were still incomplete.

"Fire the broadsides rapidly!" With this

shout, the crew began the exercise. Firing by divisions, single guns, all guns, and the cannon blasted. Delighted clapping by the ladies followed each burst. Emma shuddered at the noise, but she smiled when Jonathan pointed as a shot ricocheted, skipping and bounding up the river, throwing up beautiful jets at every contact with the water.

"We plan to invite some ladies from Columbus down to observe gunnery practice," Jonathan told her. "They tended members of the crew in the Soldier's Home Hospital there, and the officers want to show their gratitude."

"Don't show them too much gratitude." Emma pursed her lips, only half teasing.

"Ahha, you know all the ladies love me!" Jonathan cocked his head to one side with a devilish gleam in his eye. Seeing the solemn expression on her delicate face, he tilted her pink silk parasol to shield them from view and slyly kissed her cheek.

"Behave, Jonathan. Someone will see you," she murmured, giggling, feeling like a schoolgirl again. She spent a happy afternoon basking in Jonathan's attention as he whispered, teased, and found every excuse to squeeze a helpful arm around her waist or surreptitiously touch her hand.

Back at Saffold, Emma stifled a yawn. Pleasantly drowsy from the brilliant sunshine and the wind along the river, she closed her eyes from the constantly rippling shimmer. Like cold water dashed in her face, new orders were flung with a shout from the wharf. The gunboat must report to a new station fifty miles south at Chattahoochee, Florida. There at the Alabama boundary where the Chattahoochee became the Apalachicola River, work would be completed on her engines. Even though the *Chattahoochee* was helpless to maneuver, she would stand guard against the advancing enemy with her guns.

Cheers went up from men anxious for a chance at action. Suddenly chilled and drooping wearily, Emma anxiously listened to snatches of George Gift's daring plan to attack the enemy.

The dinner party that evening at The Pines was overshadowed by the fact that the *Chattahoochee* was leaving the next day. A cold, wet wind kept the guests grouped around the fireplaces. Distractedly, Jonathan and the other officers attempted light banter; however, it was obvious that their minds were upon their impending duty. Only Lieutenant Gift retreated to a quiet corner to talk earnestly with Ellen.

After the men had returned to the gunboat and the girls were braiding their hair for the night, Ellen shyly confided to Emma that George Gift had declared his undying love and proposed marriage.

"Oh, how wonderful!" Emma exclaimed. Noting Ellen's placid look, she added, "What did you tell him?"

"Well, he rather surprised me — our acquaintance has been so brief," Ellen replied quietly. "I told him about my father's prejudice against army and navy men. If he makes himself better known to my parents, who can tell? I asked him to wait a year and propose again." Ellen knelt beside the high bed in prayer; then she climbed on the step and blew out the candle.

Submerged in the soft feather bed, Emma stared through the darkness at the canopy over her head, wishing she could share Ellen's wisdom and patience. She must control her fear that love would again slip through her fingers as it had when she was young and her grandfather had refused to let her marry Michael. Her days stretched long with loneliness; her life held no purpose. She tried to recapture the joy of her day on the river, but a brooding emptiness overwhelmed her and a hard lump lodged in her chest. Dawn streaked the sky before she slept.

Tired and tense, she rubbed her neck as they reached the wharf the next morning. Pretending they felt secure from enemy attack, the ladies bid their champions good-bye and waved until the colors of the *Chattahoochee*'s flags blended with the autumn leaves drifting down the stream.

Harrison was to remain with the *Wave* at the navy yard for her plating and gun installation. Lily supervised the removal of the Chickering grand piano and some other treasures; then she patted the huge steamboat and told her good-bye. Clinging to Harrison's hand until the very last minute, she whispered, " 'The Lord watch between me and thee, when we are absent one from another.' "

Boarding a sailing vessel, *Kate L. Bruce,* bound northward to Eufaula, Lily and Emma hung over the rail and fluttered their handkerchiefs at Harrison and the *Wave* until they were out of sight. Falling into each other's arms, they burst into tears.

Panic rose in Emma's throat, and she gripped the rail fearfully as they rounded a bend. Ahead, three connected boats stretched across the river. Suddenly the boats began to tip. Passengers rushed to the rail shouting, gasping in astonishment as the muddy waters swirled over the three boats, sinking into the channel.

Jostled from her handhold, Emma barely avoided falling as the large sailing schooner lurched and careened nearly into the barrier. A thrill of fear rippled over the passengers. It had been believed that the enemy was held off downriver, but popping up along the riverbank were over a hundred men. Suddenly the colors of the Confederate Engineer Corps waved. Those who had, moments earlier, relaxed weakly, surged forward toward the captain.

"Have no fear," Captain Theodore Moreno shouted, waving his gauntlet. "We have the situation under control. I'm a civil engineer sent to partially obstruct the channel. At all costs we must keep the enemy out of Columbus, but I'll get you through." He climbed to the pilothouse, pointing out a narrow channel for the huge schooner's passage.

Word buzzed along the decks that Moreno had constructed several batteries at Columbus and another at Fort Gaines, which lay just ahead. Forewarning about the battery did little to dispel the fear produced by the sight of the body of twenty-four-pound cannon and the wagons and artillerymen.

"It's good to know they're here to protect

us," Lily said in a small, unconvincing voice as she patted her mother's hand.

Cordelia had come on deck when they stopped. The bristling cannon made her swoon. "Is the enemy really advancing up our river?" she cried.

"Oh, Lily." Emma shivered. "I felt so cut off from Jonathan when the river was too low to pass this summer. Now I understand his frustration about the placing of obstructions. Will we be cut off from them for good?"

Silently, Lily shrugged and shook her head.

"Harrison has been wounded!" Lily came running into Barbour Hall with the terrifying news. "The messenger assures me his wounds are slight. Oh, but I must go to him at once!"

"What happened?" Emma gasped.

"The *Wave* was severely damaged in battle with a Federal blockader," Lily replied. Her face paper-white against her dark hair, she continued breathlessly. "She's being towed up from Apalachicola Bay." She saw Emma's hands clutching, twisting against her chest and added, "The *Chattahoochee* is returning to Saffold for repairs. They have Harrison."

Even though the trip was becoming increasingly dangerous from the war and obstructions in the river and the onset of winter storms, Lily began hurried preparations to catch the next steamer, and Emma began to fear being left behind.

She sat beside Cordelia feeding her ginger tea for her headache, nervously awaiting her decision. Finally, Mrs. Edwards decided that she would remain, but Emma should take some warm clothing and blankets to Foy.

Cold rain was falling when their steamer reached the Saffold Navy Yard. Noticing guards on the *Chattahoochee,* they ran down the wharf.

Wet, shivering, Emma did not care who saw them as Jonathan threw his arms around her and helped her aboard the gunboat. Even though she always hated going below the waterline, she welcomed the wardroom's shelter from the wind. Lily hurried to Harrison, who lay in one of the officer's cabins.

Jonathan and Emma sat in the officers' mess drinking sassafras tea. The Wingates joined them at the oak table, Harrison pale from loss of blood.

"It's nothing," he declared of his injured shoulder. "Glad as I am to see you both,

I'm sorry, too." He sighed and shook his head. "Lily says she must see it through to the end."

"You've told her then?" queried Jonathan.

Emma lifted puzzled eyes to his face. "What?"

"The thing we've been dreading," Jonathan replied. "General Howell Cobb has taken command. He says southwest Georgia and southeast Alabama are now the granary of the Confederacy. That plus the sword factory in Columbus, and all the cotton — and — well, he's ordered Captain Moreno to obstruct the river — completely." He dropped his head in his hands and raked his fingers through his curls. "To keep the enemy out, we will bottle ourselves up."

"But they don't have to know we're bottled up," said Harrison firmly. "It's rumored that the reason they tried to capture the *Wave* is they still need light-draft steamers to engage and sink the *Chattahoochee*. We must keep them in fear of her."

Lily's liquid brown eyes overflowed with tears. "The *Wave* is what Moreno means to use," she answered Emma's questioning look.

Catesby Jones came down the ladder and greeted the guests. Rubbing his hand over his balding head and tugging at his beard, he reluctantly agreed to let Lily and Emma accompany them downriver.

Emma and Lily boarded the *Chatta-hoochee* in darkness, having left Mrs. Johnston's warm beds at five o'clock in the morning. The crew hurried things forward, bundling cumbersome traps aboard. The anchor came apeak at sunrise; the topsails were sheeted home, and the cry rang out, "All hands make sail!"

The women had barely gotten warm below deck when they were thrown from their chairs with a sudden slam. The gunboat had run ashore, twisting and straining the ship aft.

"She's leaking! Hawsers out! Man the pumps!"

The doleful *rattle, rattle, chuck, chuck* of the pumps made Lily and Emma clutch each other's hands.

Jonathan and George Gift ran the hawsers. The large ropes secured the ship while the pumps lowered the water. After about an hour the ship was freed, but by that time the wind had risen treacherously; consequently, the sails were lowered and the boilers fired.

As they steamed ahead uneventfully, Jonathan laughed and told Emma, "The crew is grumbling that we had no right to expect good luck."

She raised her eyebrows. "Because of us women on board?"

"No," he chuckled. "Because we started on Friday."

"King's Rock!" A shout rang out from above. "King's Rock!"

At this spot, twenty miles north of the town of Chattahoochee, Harrison's steamer, the *Peytona,* had been completely destroyed on the rocks when he was hurrying to his and Lily's wedding. Only Lily's deep faith that he would come had kept her family from sending the guests away.

Jonathan hurried topside again. Harrison clasped Lily's hands and joined her in prayer.

Retreating from their oneness, Emma threw a heavy shawl about her head and shoulders. If she and Jonathan were married, at least she would have a brooch, with a lock of his hair, upon her breast to hold onto. She climbed to the deck to watch as the men ran lines ashore and dropped for about a mile. Winter rains made the water deeper than when the *Peytona* and another steamer, the *Apalachicola,* had been completely wrecked; but she knew that many steamers had come to grief here regardless

189

of depth. Water rushed through the narrow channel past menacing rocks. Looking fearfully at the threatening walls of the channel, Emma shivered.

For fifteen seemingly interminable hours, officers and crew remained on deck. When finally the danger was past and they came below, their throats were so sore from yelling that they could barely speak.

The *Wave,* tied to the wharf, listing badly and with great hunks of her wedding-cake trim missing, was the first sight they saw when they reached the town of Chattahoochee, Florida.

"Oh!" Lily's voice was like the cry of an injured bird.

Theodore Moreno met them. "I've heard there's a large chain left lying on the wharf at Apalachicola," he said. "I'm going to slip into the city under cover of night and — steal it!" He gestured offhandedly as though it would be quite simple.

Jonathan's experience in slipping silently by the Federal war vessels anchored in the harbor made him a likely candidate to accompany Moreno. They and thirteen other daring men left in a small scow schooner.

Emma spent a sleepless night in the hotel, pacing the floor, visualizing the poised guns of the enemy, ready to blow the scow out of the water as if it were a bug.

The next day when the *Chattahoochee* had been refueled and scrubbed fore and aft, everyone reboarded. At the point where the river became mightier, as the Flint River, red with the mud of southwestern Georgia, poured into the Chattahoochee to become the Apalachicola River, the engines failed and no amount of work could get them going. Finally, they hoisted sails and, with guns ready, reached a series of horseshoe bends known as the Narrows. There they waited, a floating battery to guard this area on the level with the Florida capital of Tallahassee. No one dared voice the fear that the raiding party would not return to meet them.

At last the schooner sailed into sight. Fifteen men waved and shouted exuberantly.

Jonathan related their adventure gleefully. "We approached cautiously. The lights of the Yankees boats glittered on the water. We let our scow float slowly by, drifting on the current, holding our breath that they wouldn't see us. We crept up on the wharf, shouldered the chain, lowered it into the scow. *Clank!* Dropping on board, it sounded loud enough to wake the dead!" He laughed heartily.

"I'll never forget the sound," chuckled Moreno. "They must have been in their cups or they would've heard it. But we slipped right under their noses with our prize!" he said proudly.

Around the bend limped the *Wave*. Lily knew the sad moment had come. Harrison positioned the beautiful paddle wheeler across the narrowest part of the river. The prized chain was carried through her dining hall. Harrison brought out the ship's wheel. Weak from effort, he leaned on Lily as they stood on the bank. Clinging together, they watched with ashen faces as the chain was fastened.

Even while the engineers worked to hook the chain to the opposite shore, George Gift begged Captain Jones, "Don't let them block us in! When the *Chattahoochee*'s engines are repaired, we can recapture Apalachicola! We must be able to get down-river," he pleaded, "to guard the mouth against the Yankee marauders!"

Sadly, Jones pointed upward to the thirty-two-pounders being placed in a battery along Rock Bluff. "These obstructions are the main defense of the river." He shook his balding head. "There is little hope of resistance above if the enemy breaks through here!"

Crash! Crash! Crash! Emma jumped, clutching air. Felled trees crushed the *Wave*'s pilothouse, splintering the lacy hurricane deck. More timber gashed her side. The river, swollen by winter freshets, violated her decks. The crew stood at attention and saluted with Captain Harrison Wingate the sinking lady who was giving her life for their country.

Later, when Harrison silently handed Lily Captain Moreno's voucher — $1,325.35 for the *Wave*'s hull — Lily wept again.

Through icy winter rains, Harrison once again carried cargo up and down the Chattahoochee as captain of the steamboat *Alice.* Lily frequently accompanied him, leaving a lonely Emma to remain with Cordelia.

The *Chattahoochee* was formally commissioned on January 1, 1863, with Jonathan a part of her proud crew. She steamed up and down the river scanning with her guns, marking time as each side laid plans to attack the other.

Emma's days passed in a blur until the roaring March wind reminded her that on the fourteenth she would turn thirty. Elizabeth and Mollie were only a year and a half younger; yet they were respected matrons with lovely homes and beautiful children. As much as she wanted to forget her advancing age, she was a little hurt that no one remembered her birthday.

A letter from Jonathan brought a smile back to her delicate face.

CSS Chattahoochee in Florida waters
February 15, 1863

My Darling Emma,

I miss you so much. We are having a life of laborious inaction. I would sooner have the privilege of shying a shell at the rascals occasionally. When we get our ironclads finished, we shall trash them all. We have made plans for an entertainment for the ladies of Columbus who had given our men such good care in the hospital. They are to come down by steamer. They will stop at The Pines to pick up the ladies there. I will let you know the definite plans so that they can pick you up when they pass Eufaula.

Can't wait to see you,
Jonathan Ramsey

Emma washed her best frocks and made arrangements to have her hoop skirts repaired, as no new ones could be bought. The lace curtains in her room would be long enough to make a wedding dress, and she had found bits of old lace trimming in the attic. There were no buttons, but she began collecting persimmon seeds to substitute. Eagerly, she found excuses to be in town whenever mail was expected. At last her vigil was rewarded in late April with a letter.

CSS Chattahoochee in Florida waters
February 25, 1863

My Dearest Emma,

Catesby Jones has been transferred and we have a new commander, Lieutenant John Julius Guthrie. He is agreeable to go ahead with our plans for entertaining the Columbus ladies. I will let you know. We have been visited by some delightful local ladies. But you know where my heart is. George Gift has proposed a daring plan to fit up a steamboat with cotton and go down to the Apalachicola bar and pick up a Yankee craft. If his elaborate scheme works, we shall recapture Apalachicola!

> Your obedient servant,
> Jonathan Ramsey

Worry lines creased Emma's forehead. She feared Gift's harebrained schemes. She always shuddered when he bragged of the many ships sunk from under him while he swam for his life. She went to town each day in May but received no word. On the last day of the cool, wet month, she was surprised at the numbers of people she saw, all talking excitedly.

"What's happened?" she asked breathlessly.

"The *Chattahoochee* exploded! Many are wounded! Fifteen are dead!"

CHAPTER 11

"Do they have the names?" Emma gasped, her voice echoing hollowly against the buzzing in her ears. No one seemed to hear her question. Shimmering spots before her eyes blinded her. Groping, she found a box and sat heavily. When finally she thought she could stand without fainting, she plucked at the sleeve of the man who had brought the terrible news.

"Please, please, Sir." She swallowed and wavered again. "My husband-to-be was aboard — do — do you have —" Her delicate face went beyond pallor to blueness. "Do you know the names of the wounded — the — the — dead?"

The big, gruff man looked down at her, grabbed off his hat, and replied, "No'm, ain't heard who's dead. Only know fourteen — maybe fifteen — was killed when the thing blowed up. Three drowned." He brightened. "I hear tell Lieutenant Guthrie, he run about the deck administering baptism to the dying. Was he . . ."

Emma shook her head.

"Dr. Ford give aid t' th' scalded."

Again she shook her head, unable to speak.

"Them's the only names I heard." His ruddy face broke into a hopeful smile. "But many of the wounded abandoned ship — jumped right overboard afore she sank. Happened on May twenty-seventh at high noon. 'Tis said they laid on the muddy banks in the pouring rain from then 'til midnight when that old steamer *William H. Young* came and carried 'em away."

"Carried them?" Emma swallowed. "Carried them where?"

"Well, Ma'am." He twisted his hat in his hand. "The dead was taken to Chattahoochee for burial. Some wounded —" he scratched his head and spat tobacco juice — "might be at Saffold, but lots of the worst 'uns was taken to that there hospital in Columbus. You know, the Soldier's Home."

"Thank you," she whispered and turned away. Her tears frozen, she staggered toward home, her knees giving way again and again as she climbed the hill to Barbour Hall. Stopping several times to rest, she tried frantically to decide how to tell Cordelia;

but her thoughts bumped against the hard, cold hollows of her insides, and she could not capture them.

As gently as she could, she explained the tragedy to her sister-in-law. Crying in each other's arms, they tried to decide whether to go upstream or down. They agreed to go to Saffold; then, they doubted their choice. If only the Wingates had been at home — Harrison would know how best to travel; Lily would pray for guidance. Finally, they decided time enough had passed for the steamer to have reached Columbus with the load of wounded. Holding fast to the hope that their loved ones were alive, they chose to go first to the hospital, last to the cemetery.

The slowness of the journey tortured Emma. She sat in a little heap, congealed into numbness. Trying to shut out the sound of Cordelia's fits of loud blubbering and her piteous recounting of the tale to every stranger they met, Emma thought the trip would never end.

When they arrived at the Soldier's Home on the southwest corner of Broad and Thomas Streets, they walked past carriages jamming both avenues that led to the wooden building. Going through the first floor, pressing her fist against her mouth and swallowing convulsively, Emma looked from one man to another, burned almost beyond recognition. *Jonathan and Foy are alive. They must be alive,* she told herself over and over to fill the emptiness of her soul.

Blinking tears, fighting nausea, she grasped the loose flesh of Cordelia's elbow and helped the puffing old woman upstairs. "Why?" Emma cried bitterly. "Why does God let things like this happen?"

"Mama!" A weak gasp stopped them midway through the upper floor.

With tears of joy, Cordelia sank to the cot and gathered Foy in her arms.

"Oh, Mama," Foy sobbed against her shoulder, "my friend Mallory's feet and hands are crisped; his face is badly scalded." He snuffed and struggled for control. "But he's so cheerful. He'll make it — he was a hero on the *Virginia* — he must make it!"

Shivering, Emma waited to be certain Foy was not critically injured before she asked about Jonathan. Scrubbing his finger under his nose, he pointed to a corner.

Jonathan was sleeping. Emma thought he had never looked so beautiful. His matted curls shone darkly against the pallor of his face, gone slack like a small boy's. Shaking with relief, she collapsed to a stool and sat quietly beside him, content to watch him breathe.

"Ma'am," a weak voice whispered from the cot behind her. "I'm Duffey," he gasped as she turned. "Fireman — *Chattahoochee* — please — read." Then he rolled his eyes in the direction of a small table.

Emma picked up the Bible he indicated and began to read Psalms. Her lips stiff with the horror of his burns, she merely called the words. Soothed, he fell asleep.

She sat gazing at Jonathan. No burns marred his skin. Her hand hovered about him as she restrained her longing to touch him. She leaned over to examine his left foot, wrapped in a bloody bandage.

Jonathan's eyelids fluttered. Noticing her, he sat bolt upright. "Oh, Em — I hate for you to see . . ." Weakly, he fell back. "It's too — it's too terrible." Jerking wildly, his hand groped for hers.

Quietly, she caught his hand in both of hers and whispered soothing words. Brushing a quick kiss across his fevered brow, she looked up and saw a well-groomed woman smiling at her. Gratefully, Emma reached for the bowl of milk and bread she held out. She had heard that the ladies of Columbus were feeding their own families corn bread and saving their precious store of flour for the soldiers' bread. As she tenderly fed the warm milk to Jonathan, the edges of her heart began to melt.

Strengthened by the milk toast, Jonathan talked wildly, as if ripping the words from his brain. "It was so terrible," he repeated, wiping his arm across his eyes. "Those scalded men ran — ran about — about the deck, frantic with pain, leaving the impression of their bleeding feet — sometimes flesh — the nails and all — behind them." He gagged. "After the boilers exploded, we . . . thought the magazine would blow, too. Men were going over the side." He choked.

"Don't think about it." Emma patted him. "It's over. It's over." She pushed him back against the pillow and wished that she could gather him in her arms as Cordelia had done Foy.

"I wouldn't mind so much if we had taken out the enemy." He raised toward her on one elbow and would not let her soothe him back. "Let me tell you. The schooner *Fashion* was loaded — it was loaded with cotton — trying to run the blockade — Indian Pass. Captured, and we tried . . . ," he coughed but kept talking jerkily, "to cross the obstructions, give aid. The river was too low to cross Blountstown Bar. We waited.

202

Waited for the river to rise. The order was given to raise steam, and then — and then . . ."

"Was this Mr. Gift's plan?" Emma wondered frantically how to get Jonathan's mind off of the horrifying scene.

"No." He swallowed hard and recovered himself. "No, George had gone to General Cobb's headquarters for approval. We could have recaptured Apalachicola." He gasped and fell back weakly, "but now the *Chattahoochee* is no more." Tears slipped between his tightly squeezed eyelids.

"Rest now. Rest," she soothed. "We're going to stay with Cordelia's sister, Laurie. I'll be here." She wet her handkerchief and washed the offending tears, smoothed back the damp curls. "Sleep now. I'll be here every day. Just sleep."

"They're burying Duffey in Linwood Cemetery." Jonathan sighed, reaching for Emma's hand when she returned the next morning. Foy wept quietly. His fellow midshipman, Charles Mallory, had also died.

Emma felt that Jonathan would have recovered his strength more quickly if she had had salt to season the food she cooked daily and brought to him. It angered her when she heard that the enemy had learned that the *Chattahoochee* had sunk and had attacked the saltworks on Alligator Bay, east of Dog Island, scattering two hundred bushels of salt along the shore.

One afternoon Emma looked up from reading to her listless patient to see Lieutenant Gift, greeting everyone cheerily, bouncing across the room, stirring disheveled, disconsolate men to life with his immaculate uniform and exuberant manner.

"Great news, men," he sang out. "We're raising the *Chattahoochee!*"

Hoarse voices cheered.

"I placed the Dahlgren," he said as he moved beside Jonathan's cot, "and one of the thirty-two-pounders as a battery on the riverbank where she lies. Just in time, too." He gestured excitedly. "The Union heard she was out of commission. They tried to pass the Narrows," he nodded at Emma, "where the *Wave* lies." He paused until the effect of the enemy attack soaked into opium-dazed brains. "General Cobb dispatched a force to strengthen us. The Federals didn't expect the *Chattahoochee*'s guns to be breathing down upon them from the bluff," he laughed. "We sent 'em packing!"

The room filled with clapping and cheering.

"You can salvage her, then?" Jonathan's eyes lighted with interest, and he raised on one elbow to question his friend.

"Yes," Gift assured him. "The job's tremendous, but David S. Johnston is towing her to Saffold for overhauling. We'll have her back in service in no time."

Jonathan struggled to regain his strength. Floundering weakly, he finally mastered heavy crutches. Though she worried over the cause — his foot remained a bloody, draining, putrid-smelling sore — Emma rejoiced that he was unable to be transferred to Savannah with the uninjured of his crew. When the Saffold Navy Yard repaired the damage to the *Chattahoochee*'s timbers, she was to be brought to Columbus for replacement of machinery and boilers. Jonathan would still be there.

Nervously, she watched his color improve and his strength increase; however, she searched in vain for the return of his high spirits and unflagging good humor. Thinking that sunshine would help him, Emma proposed a carriage ride. As they left the hospital behind and she threw back her head and breathed deeply of the fragrant summer air, Jonathan squeezed her hand in his old loving way. For so long he had clutched it, as if silently begging for strength she did not have to give. The dreadful fear that he would not recover melted slightly, but her face felt stiff as she smiled at him. Words would not come, so they rode silently. Lost in whirling worries, she did not notice their direction until he reined the horse at the Columbus Naval Yard.

George Gift waved to them. Although she murmured protests, Jonathan struggled with his cumbersome crutches and made his way across the yard, panting.

"Our ram is progressing!" exclaimed Gift, tipping his hat to Emma as they joined him. "The boilers are in and the engines are ready to set." He smiled at Emma and explained, "The *Muscogee* is patterned after the *Merrimack/Virginia*. When we get her launched, the enemy will know we'll give 'em a fight."

Emma looked at the wide, flat boat made of square, green pine and tried to understand as he showed her that it was placed solidly instead of in ribs like an ordinary boat. A great many men were pounding huge iron nails, while others were busily caulking. Her spirits lifted on the swell of Gift's enthusiasm.

"The iron for plating is scarce, so it might be November before we launch." Gift shrugged. "But soon as our ironclads on the Alabama are finished and in action, we'll easily repossess New Orleans. The news coming from the Mississippi River is good!" Eyebrows raised, he bobbed about as he spoke. "Many think this is the turning point of the war. The campaign at Vicksburg will close gloriously for us." He threw up his hand dramatically. "I'd say, within the next ten days!"

Jonathan straightened on his crutches. A broad smile spread across his face. His dark eyes came alive again. Laughing for the first time in weeks, he looked at Emma tenderly and renewed his promise with a slow and deliberate wink.

Emma's spirits soared.

Declaring a crushed foot could not keep him down, Jonathan resumed his duty. Reluctantly, Emma told him good-bye. With Cordelia and the convalescing Foy, she returned to Eufaula.

They found the population swelled with refugees from Vicksburg, speaking with the same optimism George Gift had voiced. Emma cleaned Barbour Hall in happy preparation for a celebration visit from Jonathan.

With total shock they received the news from Vicksburg. On July fourth, the Confederate stronghold, which had controlled the Mississippi River, had fallen. The Confederate States were divided.

The fall of Vicksburg plunged Eufaulians into despair. Emma stood in the marketplace washed in a pitch and yaw of anguished words. The townspeople had believed the city to be well supplied with food and ammunition. Now, four days after the fall, they learned the brave garrison had lived for two weeks by eating their horses and mules, finally surrendering because men were dying of starvation.

She was asked to help nurse several of the refugee children, victims of whooping cough, who had come to Eufaula. They died; despair had no end. The summer of 1863 seemed blotchy with measles and smallpox, blotting out worry about the increasingly bad war news.

"Why does God let these horrible things happen?" an exhausted Emma flung at Lily as they sat on the porch one steaming afternoon.

Lily closed her eyes for a long moment before she replied. "God doesn't cause the evil in the world," she answered softly. "Men do. With their sinful, greedy ways."

"But Christians suffer just as much — sometimes more." Emma dropped her head between sweaty palms. "Don't you ever wish you could just run away?"

Lily tried to hug her, but Emma's shoulders remained stiff. "Darling Emma, Jesus told His disciples they would have to face trials and tribulations, but they could live victoriously if they would completely commit their lives to trusting and obeying Him."

Emma glared at her; a muscle twitched in her cheek. She did not reply because Lily simply could not understand; she thought that everything could fit into what she called the lordship of Christ.

"We couldn't do much good if we ran away — if we withdrew from the world." Lily continued to speak sweetly, ignoring Emma's silence. "A boat must be in the water to be of any use. Each Christian is given a task to help others find safe harbor in the storms."

A contemptuous laugh twisted Emma's mouth. "Well, my ship is tossing on a mighty stormy sea."

"But, don't you understand? If you'll just ask, God will send His Spirit, the very presence of Jesus, to walk beside you, to guide and strengthen. Oh, Emma, don't try to live your life alone!"

Emma turned away from her and walked into the dry, wilting garden. She had always walked alone. It seemed she always would. Jonathan remained at Columbus supervising the repair of the *Chattahoochee* and the building of the *Muscogee.* She knew that his foot refused to heal. It still drained and caused him pain, but he hobbled about on crutches. His letters remained full of plans for an offensive. Columbus, the head of navigation in the Apalachicola-Chattahoochee River system, was the last stronghold in Confederate naval installations. Emma knew with a sickening dread that Confederate naval efforts could be driven in no farther north than Columbus, Georgia.

Christmas scented the air. Jonathan's eyes sparkled, and his voice held its old excitement as he arrived at Barbour Hall to take Emma to the Christmas Eve party at Roseland Plantation. "We're ready to launch the *Muscogee!*" he said. "We're only waiting for the river to rise, and from present appearances that won't be long!"

Smilingly Emma listened, enjoyed being near him, and reveled in the fact that they could sit side by side for five miles through the clear, star-filled night. When they arrived at Roseland's gates, Emma noticed that many other officers and soldiers were in the buggies and carriages circling the glistening, white sand driveway. Colonel and Mrs. Toney, who now owned the beautiful white house, greeted their guests with aristocratic manners and urged all to make merry.

Emma did not mind sitting at the edge of the room while others danced; however, the lilting rhythm of the "Tallahassee Waltz" made her feet step and glide automatically beneath her hoop skirt.

"We could make it a threesome — you, my crutch, and me." Jonathan's face contorted with the first bitterness Emma had seen him show.

"How in the world do you suppose they were able to load the table with so many delicacies?" interrupted Elizabeth Rhodes, sitting down beside them with her beloved Chauncey. "I really do not approve of giving such entertainments with our country in such dire distress." Elizabeth sniffed disdainfully. "Christmas Day will be sad with so many chairs left vacant with occupants fallen on a bloody field . . ."

Emma's wan smile became a mask, and she shut out her friend's sad pronouncements. Her happiness could not be dampened, because the launching of the *Muscogee* was near, and Jonathan had invited her to come.

Icy wind cut through Emma's cashmere shawl and scratched its fingers under the frayed bands of navy blue ribbon in the club trim on her faded pink coat and skirt. The wool was shiny now, wearing thin, and Emma had difficulty trying to keep her teeth from chattering as she stood with the crowd on the banks of the Chattahoochee at the Naval Ironworks in Columbus for the launching of the *Muscogee.* The river had risen rapidly since Christmas, ten feet just yesterday, and now on New Year's Day, 1864, the boisterous crowd waited for the ironclad ram to float from the blocks.

"Cold enough for hog killing, for sure," said the man on her left. "It's . . ."

Suddenly a brass band struck up, "When Johnny Comes Marching Home Again." Toes began to tap and scattered voices took up the popular new song, shouting out when they came to "Hurrah, Hurrah!"

Emma's eyes were on Jonathan. Proudly, without his crutch, he limped about as the crew tried to slide the *Muscogee* off the building ways and into the water. The freshet had raised the level of the water around the vessel. The added rainwater formed, pushed. For a long breath it seemed the ram must lift. The *Muscogee* held fast. The river fell back, too weak, too low. A moan went up from the crowd.

Disgusted muttering rumbled with the steamer, *Marianna,* as she was brought about to tow the ironclad into the water. Emma clutched her fists to her chest and leaned forward, still hopeful. The flat, iron ram refused to budge.

"It'll take a second flood to lift that slantin' p'cu'lar-lookin' craft," scoffed a young man wearing a badge from the *Columbus Daily Enquirer.*

Shivering, Emma waited silently for Jonathan after the crowd had dispersed. He limped toward her. The sparkle in his eyes had been replaced by grim determination.

"We'll have to extend her hull to add buoyancy," he said. "We may even have to reduce the casement to remove excess weight." He sighed heavily. Forcing his sagging face to lift, he grinned crookedly at her. "But we'll do it! Have faith in me, Emma. We'll break the blockade. Then I'll get you a wedding gown from Paris."

"Oh, Jonathan, I–I don't need — I have curt . . ." Her hands flew to her throat. "I have faith in you." Emma smiled sadly. Her eyes went beyond him down to the wharf to the wreck of the *Chattahoochee* listing badly to port.

Confederate victories in the spring campaigns had Eufaulians talking optimistically again, but to Emma, the failure to launch the *Muscogee* seemed an ill omen. Jonathan wrote her enthusiastic letters about the repair work on both vessels. Excitedly, he reported that Lieutenant Gift had been transferred in March to command the *Chattahoochee.*

"With Gift in charge, we can be sure of action," he wrote.

Coping with shortages filled Emma's waiting. The "coffee" she made by roasting sweet potatoes and okra seed was as unsatisfying as her pretense at living. Woodenly waiting upon Cordelia, she existed between letters, until April gowned herself in dainty bridal wreath spirea and tossed on honeysuckle veils. The love songs of the birds, as they worked companionably on their nests, struck a responsive chord in Emma's heart and plucked forth embarrassing spasms of tears.

The green velvet skirt of May mushroomed around Barbour Hall as they stepped onto the porch early one morning. Emma strained forward as she heard a muffled shout.

"A gunboat!" The words trembled on the breeze.

"A gunboat! At the wharf!" echoed through deserted streets.

"A gunboat! The Yankees!" gasped Cordelia, sagging in a swoon.

"A gunboat! The *Chattahoochee*?" shouted Emma expectantly. Leaving Cordelia to Kitty, she ran to the stable and hitched the pony to the buggy by herself. Wielding a whip with one hand and clutching the careening buggy with the other, she reached the wharf completely disheveled, but she did not care.

The stone-colored gunboat lay smartly at the wharf with flags flying. Beaming, Jonathan saluted Emma from the gun deck. Dabbing her hair into place, she hurried to meet him at the gangway.

How she longed to fly into his arms, but crowds of people were converging to gawk at the *Chattahoochee.* Jonathan's hands hovered close to her shoulders, and the transmitted warmth told her he shared her yearning.

As if to restrain himself, he quickly grasped both her hands. Vibrant again, he smiled into her eyes with the impact of a touch and whispered, "Emma, my darling!"

"Oh, Jonathan," she breathed. "Jonathan."

Speaking his name brought such joy. For one long moment they existed alone. Then jostling elbows made her look around at the scrubbed deck, the replaced cannon. "Oh, is she repaired?" Her voice came out a high squeak. "Are you on the way to break the blockade at last?"

"Well, yes," Jonathan grinned sheepishly, "and no." He guided her to a less crowded spot beside the smokestack before he explained. "She's repaired — but empty." He turned his palms up expressively. "We have no iron to build engines or boilers. We just let her drift down the river. We got her here safely only through Harrison Wingate's expertise as pilot. We kept her in the channel by using sweeps."

"Sweeps?" Disappointment flattened her tone, and she sagged against the smokestack.

"Long oars. To turn her bow into the current."

"Oh." She turned away so that he could not see her face. "Then why did you leave Columbus?"

"The river above is almost dried up. The water level is so low we were afraid she'd break her back. We planned to go farther, but she grounded twice, and we'll have to leave her at Eufaula until another rise in the river."

"Then you're going . . ."

"Gift is in command." His eyes glittered with excitement. "George has a daring plan to break the blockade — but come below where it's quieter."

As Emma stepped below deck into the wardroom, Ellen Shackelford emerged from the captain's cabin. Emma's shock could not be disguised. "Ellen — I–I didn't know you were here," she stammered.

The dainty girl blushed. "Then you haven't heard the news?"

Emma shook her head.

"Mr. Gift and I were married at The Pines on the tenth of April."

Emma hugged her friend; but jealousy's icy steel plunged hard between them, muffling her good wishes. She had heard that Hannah had married Myles Collier last September. All the officers were finding time for marriage — except Jonathan.

That evening, she brushed her hair until it shone, then donned her pink organdy and Jonathan's rubies. Smilingly, she gave him her hand when he called for her to attend the frolic on board the *Chattahoochee*. Pleasantly, she laughed at his jokes as she nibbled refreshments. Sweetly, she joined in the singing of "The Last Rose of Summer," "Home Sweet Home," and "Annie Laurie."

But the high vibrating whine of a Jew's harp floated plaintively on the still air, making it impossible to keep back her tears any longer. Perhaps Jonathan did not really love her. She moved down the deck from him, unnoticed. With a shuddering sigh, she let the thought escape which she had fought to suppress. Jonathan had never actually said the words, "I love you." She sank into a chair. The music stopped.

"Here's the plan," George Gift announced exuberantly. "Our valiant lady cannot take us into the fray without her boilers." Waving his hand over his head, he shouted, "But her crew will win her honor! Tomorrow at dawn we leave for the bay, taking all of the ship's boats and . . ."

Emma turned questioning eyes on Jonathan, but he was watching Gift.

"My force will consist of 130 men and officers," Gift was saying. "I shall bring all my young men back lieutenants," he boasted. High-spirited shouts applauded him.

"We will attack at East Pass," he continued in a lower conspiratorial voice. "The coast is blockaded by the U.S. steamers *Somerset* and *Adela.* In our ship's boats, we will slip up on one, man her, and capture the other. Then, we'll run the vessels into Mobile — or burn them!"

Feet stamped; hands clapped; cheers sounded.

In lonely silence, Emma sat with fear pounding in her temples. Feeling she must get away from the noise, she moved to the bow of the boat. Jonathan followed.

"What a daring — and dangerous — scheme!" she breathed fearfully.

"Isn't it?" Jonathan grinned delightedly. "We're a crew without a ship. What else can we do?"

"Nothing. But you can't fight with courage alone," she said flatly.

"We have incendiary materials, rifles, muskets, shotguns, revolvers, and cutlasses . . ."

"Oh, yes," she said sourly, "you have guns." She laughed bitterly. "And what did they say the *Somerset* had — ten cannon?" She turned away from him. Angry with herself that she could not stop the tears streaming down her cheeks, she gritted her teeth. "You'll attack a giant warship with a rowboat!"

"Don't you worry your pretty head," he said gently, turning her face toward him. "We can do it with surprise on our side.

They'll never expect it!" He caressed her cheek and stroked away the tears. "I'll soon be back a hero — and then . . ."

Pain seared her inside, and she could not keep it out of her eyes as she searched his face. For so many years she had ached with emptiness. No one cared about her. Oh, why had she let herself love him so desperately?

Jonathan dropped a light, teasing kiss upon her trembling lips. When she neither responded nor fussed that someone might see, he studied her thoughtfully. "It's more than our mission, isn't it? I thought you looked angry and hurt with me when you found out George and Ellen were married." He plunged his fingers into his hair and squeezed his palms against his forehead.

For a long, silent moment they stood motionless, with distance growing between them. Then he began to speak slowly, deliberately, "I'm not like him. George flies off in all directions at once. In the midst of all this, he's been on a daring adventure on the *Ranger* from Bermuda to the Wilmington Bar. He survived another wreck and came back feeling wealthy."

He snorted and looked the other way. Continuing in a gruff voice he said, "I have nothing. No money at all. My funds are tied up at my plantation. Anyway, I guess I can just handle one thing at a time." His voice dropped despondently. "We have so little left to fight with. We've got to break this blockade or all is lost." Throwing up his hands, he set his dark curls standing up on end. "Can't you give me just a little more time?"

"Yes." Demurely she bowed her head, and moonlight washed her hair with silver. "I'm sorry I was so . . . I . . ." Fragile as the moths fluttering about the ship's lantern, she quivered and seemed about to fly away.

Jonathan pulled her into a shadow and wrapped her in his arms. The passionate strength of his kisses was all of the promise she needed to set her heart hoping again.

The next morning at dawn, Emma stood on the wharf watching. The crew marched off the proud *Chattahoochee,* turned, saluted. They ambled aboard the riverboat, *Marianna.* Her yawls and those of the steamers *Young* and *Uchee* and one metallic boat were tucked beneath her wings. Dragging behind her were the two boats belonging to the *Chattahoochee.* Like a mother hen taking her biddies to attack the hawk, this pitiful fleet left the dock.

"Foolhardy!" snorted Cordelia.

Saying nothing, Emma leaned forward,

hand stretched out motionlessly toward the gay flags fluttering from the *Marianna*. Jonathan shouted something, but behind him the band was playing. She stood until the last sad notes of the trumpet sang, "I'll take my stand, to live and die in Dixie. Away . . ."

The steamboat rounded the bend. Silence engulfed the wharf. Silence filled the days. Silence and an agony of waiting.

CHAPTER 12

"Shipwrecked! As our whole nation is, it seems." Harrison Wingate sat in the parlor of Barbour Hall with his head in his hands.

Emma had never seen the vital man defeated. Her emotions churning, she sat silently, fighting for outer calm and biting her tongue to keep from shouting her questions as he related their disaster with agonizing detail — but her mind was screaming.

"We tried valiantly," he resumed slowly. "The *Marianna* took us to the obstructions. We carried our small boats overland around them, then drifted down the river to the bay. Muffling our oars, we landed in the night at East Point near the U.S. steamer, *Adela*." His eyes, dark hollows in his strained face, searched theirs for understanding. "Our only hope of capturing her was to board in sudden surprise. We hid our boats and waited —" he swallowed — "waited for a dark night. But every night was clear. The sea was so smooth, so phosphorescent, that when we dipped the oars into the water, they emitted a luminous light which shone brightly across the bay."

Again he dropped his head, and the ladies waited for him to resume his story. Emma wanted to cry out Jonathan's name, but her throat constricted with a burning, bitter taste. Harrison Wingate's failure to mention him inflamed her fears.

"Waiting for a stormy night to cover us," Harrison continued wearily, "we ran out of provisions. Our scouts slipped into Apalachicola. Some of our men were captured, but one scout made it back to tell us a spy had alerted the enemy of our planned attack."

Emma remembered with bitterness George Gift's loud bragging. Harrison's voice thumped dully against her roaring ears.

"Without surprise, a handful of men in rowboats had no chance," he sighed. "We pushed across the sound to escape upriver. Part of our boats hugged the shore. One under command of Midshipman DeBlanc, and one I was in under Gift, pushed directly across the sound. The enemy drove De-Blanc's force back into the swamps. Some were captured; most escaped. Part of the men went right up the river road because the Yankees mistook them for their own command." He laughed ironically.

Emma could bear it no longer. "What of Jonathan?" she squeaked.

Harrison nodded gravely. "A launch gave chase to us, but our boat was swift. We escaped the Yankees only to be caught in a stormy gale. Jonathan's boat was swamped."

Emma drew in her breath. Two red spots shone in her cheeks.

"Gift turned back to rescue them."

She exhaled, leaning forward, and clutched at Harrison's hand to drag the story from him.

"Jonathan and nine others clung to the side of our boat. Seventeen were already inside. The sea washed over us — nearly swamped us. Gift became ill. Midshipman Scharf took command. Our only hope of safety was to turn 'round and go to sea before the wind. We had to lighten the boat, so guns, water casks, supplies were thrown overboard. Five who were exhausted were taken in." He nodded at Emma. "Jonathan among them."

Lily shrank close beside Harrison.

"As we headed our boat for the Gulf of Mexico, a large wave struck under her quarter. The breakers were roaring over the beach. We threw off our clothing preparing to swim. Somehow Scharf beached us on Saint George Island."

Cordelia sighed and murmured.

"And Jonathan?" Emma managed weakly.

"Exhausted!" he exclaimed. "For two days we starved, eating palmetto cabbage, alligators, and oysters. The old wound on his foot opened up and . . ." He shook his head sadly. "He's back in the hospital in Columbus."

Emma scarcely listened to the rest of the tale of DeBlanc's search of the islands and the rescue. They had escaped upriver, sunk their boats, and traveled overland to join their party above the obstructions. Gift was back at work repairing the *Chattahoochee* and planning to try again to take the Bay, but Jonathan and a few others were in the Soldier's Home. Alive. Not dead. He was alive but very ill.

Emma prowled the room, fiddling with small objects. *How,* she wondered, *can I manage to get to Columbus?* Even though the war had relaxed some social standards, a maiden lady could not make such a trip alone. Morning sickness had plagued Lily lately, suggesting that another confinement was upon her. Emma loved Lily too much to envy her, yet the thought of another baby increased her depression that she would never have one of her own.

"How long, O Lord, before this ends?" Cordelia's wail broke through Emma's thoughts.

"What do the men say now?" asked Lily. "Those who thought this war a duel which would soon settle an affair of honor and principle with little shedding of blood?"

"Even men like Gift who were trained for warfare are saying we must arbitrate more intelligently." Harrison sighed. "War is so futile — settling a dispute by who can kill the most men solves nothing. No one ever thought there could be such a long and bloody war!"

No word came from Jonathan. On the seventeenth of June, the *Uchee* came to tow the *Chattahoochee* back to the Columbus. Emma endured the waiting, the hoping, for two more weeks before going to ask Elizabeth Rhodes to journey with her to the hospital. Elizabeth, however, was all astir over another trip. A train trip to Georgia was planned, with Colonel Shorter and his family, to visit Mrs. Shorter's brother who was in command of a brigade at Camp Sumter at a village called Andersonville — it was said that twenty-seven thousand

Yankee prisoners were confined there —
and to call upon Sophronia Bearden at
Looking Glass Plantation.

One hot afternoon, Kitty announced that
Dr. C. J. Pope and Dr. W. H. Thornton had
come to call upon Emma. Puzzled, she hurried into the parlor.

"We need you, Miss Emma," said Dr.
Pope immediately. His well-mannered tone
made a request, but his substance and self-
assurance gave import of command. "We
need you as a nurse."

Astounded, Emma stared at him. "Uh —"
She fidgeted with her collar. "Uh, do — be
seated, gentlemen." She sank to a chair.

"Wounded are pouring into Eufaula." Dr.
Thornton nodded his graying head. "We've
heard you helped out at the Soldier's Home.
We beg your aid. The Tavern on the bluff
has been turned into the ward for the blood
poison cases."

"Blood poison?" Emma's stomach turned.
She stared glassily at the frock-coated
gentlemen and stammered. "I–I'm afraid
you misunderstood. I only visited a patient.
I'm not a nurse." Remembering how she
could not look at Jonathan's wound, much
as she loved him, she swallowed bile, "I–I've
only nursed sick children." She passed her
hand over her eyes. "I really get quite

queasy . . ."

Dr. Pope pursed his lips. "Perhaps the rheumatism cases at Bell Hospital," he interjected hurriedly. "All our Confederate surgeons are transferring their chronic cases here. Surgeon H. V. Miller is treating them with a good galvanic battery and using colchium and iodide of potassium as standby remedies. We really —"

"Emma! Em-ma!" Cordelia's voice called.

Glad to hear Cordelia's summons for once, Emma rose, dismissing them. "Thank you for thinking of me, gentlemen, but my sister-in-law needs me constantly."

"Yes — ahem — do consider it," said Dr. Pope.

"We really do need you, Ma'am," agreed Dr. Thornton, hat in hand.

A letter from Jonathan came at last:

Columbus, Georgia
July 5, 1864

Dear Emma,

Don't come to Columbus. Works have been erected and every able-bodied man enlisted for the city's defense. The population has swelled to 12,000 because refugees are pouring in from north of here. Women and children are shel-

229

tered in huts and in abandoned rolling stock along the railroad. They are living on cornmeal supplied by the state.

A battery of four guns has been placed on the *William H. Young,* and some of our crew are using the old steamer to defend the river down at Chattahoochee, Florida. The *Kate L. Bruce* has been sunk as another obstruction.

We are cheered by the progress on the *Muscogee* which is nearly ready for launching. Two boilers have been sent from the wreck of the *Raleigh* at Wilmington and are being placed on the *Chattahoochee.* She will soon be ready for action. Every preparation is being made for a raid on the blockade.

Again, do not try to come here.

Your obedient servant,
Jonathan Ramsey

Emma read the letter over and over again, finding none of Jonathan's usual humor, no words of affection. Reading it yet another time, she realized he had not mentioned his wound or said where he was or what he was doing.

Her reverie was interrupted by visitors at the door. Kitty announced Mary Elizabeth Young and Dr. Hamilton Weedon.

"Emma, Dear," Mary said breathlessly as she entered the parlor with a swishing of petticoats. "May I present to you Dr. Weedon, who's been serving as chief surgeon with the Fourth Florida Regiment," she gushed, "and has just arrived to take charge of the military hospital which has been set up in the Tavern."

A slightly built man with closely cropped hair and a mustache bowed correctly over Emma's hand. He murmured polite acknowledgments and then fixed her with piercing dark eyes and spoke intensely. "I see immediately, Ma'am, that Miss Mary is correct in telling me your pleasant smile and calm manner would serve greatly in nursing desperate men."

Flustered, Emma sat down suddenly and stammered, "I'm — not at all sure that I could . . ."

"Competent nurses are hard to find," Dr. Weedon continued briskly. "So many don't know castor oil from a gun rod or laudanum from a hole in the ground."

Emma laughed shakily.

"Women make better nurses than the enlisted men." His snapping eyes assessed her, and his crisp voice demanded attention. "I'm certain you are familiar with the work of Miss Florence Nightingale during the Crimean War. When she arrived in Turkey, she cut the hospital death rate from 42 percent to 2 percent."

"I understand that she still campaigns for hospital reforms from her invalid's bed," drawled Mary, preening her brown hair. Her eyes sparkled when she looked at Dr. Weedon.

His smile softened upon her, but he whirled back to Emma. "You'd help morale. These men have wounds that will not heal. They are facing amputation — or death."

"My sister-in-law suffers terribly from rheumatism, and I spend a great deal of time nursing her . . . ," Emma whispered, wondering desperately how to defend herself from this intense man.

"Yes. Well, you have more experience for the cases at Bell Hospital." He cleared his throat. "But we can use older ladies there." He shrugged. "Those who'd get emotional or faint at the Tavern."

Cordelia Edwards swept into the parlor at that moment. Introductions and polite comments were made. When Cordelia was apprised of the situation, she shocked Emma by saying, "Of course, you may go. We must give our all for the war effort." She smiled benignly, and her chins shook importantly.

"Thank you, Miss Cordelia." Dr. Weedon

bowed gallantly. "May I beg your aid? The use of your flower garden?"

Puffed with pride, she replied, "Most certainly, but how . . ."

"As you know, the Union government has declared medicine and surgical instruments contraband of war. Our blockade-runners are no longer getting through with quinine, chloroform, morphine, paregoric —" He turned his hands to suggest emptiness. "None of the things we need so much."

Cordelia clutched her head at the mention of the lack of quinine but did not interrupt.

"Our druggists have compounded a tincture of dogwood, poplar, and willow barks mixed with whiskey as a quinine substitute." He shook his head and clucked his tongue. "It is inferior; however, the opium we've extracted from red garden poppies does help relieve the suffering. We're asking the ladies to grow them."

Emma's mind rushed on frantically as they discussed native roots and herbs Cordelia could contribute. As soon as the guests left Barbour Hall, Emma hurried to Lily's house. Pale and wan, she sat holding Mignonne and the huge family Bible.

"You're not trying to teach a four year old to read the Bible, are you?" Emma asked scornfully.

"Not yet," laughed Lilly. "I'm teaching her letters from the large capitals at the beginning of passages. But don't scoff, Emma, Dear. If you'll just listen, the voice of God will speak to you from the pages of the Bible."

Ready to change the subject, Emma explained Dr. Weedon's request. Pacing about the room, she spoke distractedly. "I've read that Florence Nightingale felt that God called her to devote her life to nursing — that she even refused to marry a man she loved because it would interfere with her dedication to duty." Her stomach gurgled and she shuddered. "I'm not called!" Her mouth twisted sourly.

"Possibly not," agreed Lily, "but your sweet, calm manner . . ."

"My calm manner," Emma laughed bitterly, "is a farce. My insides are tossing, churning — oh, Lily, I wish I had some of your inner strength," she wailed.

The next morning, Emma reported to the Tavern on the bluff high above the Chattahoochee. Shaking, she stepped across the narrow porch and stood in the doorway with her willowy body wavering as if she would fall. The three large rooms which ran across the front of the old riverboat inn were filled with cots on which lay maimed men. Low moans came from dim corners. The odor rising on waves of the intense July heat filled her mouth with bitter, sickening juice.

A large, motherly woman bustled toward her. "Good morning." She smiled. Wiping her hands on a white apron stained with blood, she reached out toward Emma and said heartily, "You must be Emma Edwards. I'm so thankful to see you, my dear. I'm Sorie Stow."

"Yes, Ma'am," Emma whispered. She swallowed hard and managed, "Mrs. Stow, I'm really not a nurse — I . . ."

The kindly woman gently guided her back onto the porch and fanned her with fresh air. "You'll get used to it, Dear. The gangrene hospitals are the worst."

"But, how do you keep from fainting — from —" she gagged — "being sick?"

Mrs. Stow looked at Emma's blue face thoughtfully and replied, "Well, I guess none of us accept it naturally. It's just something you have to fight. At first it's hard. There's a war going on between the two natures within you. But you can do it because you know it's expected of you."

Emma sighed doubtfully.

"You'll do fine." She patted Emma fondly. "Just get a smile on that pretty face. I'll let you start by taking the stronger patients out on the upstairs porch for fresh air and lemonade."

In a state of numbness, Emma stumbled through the morning with a false smile and shaking hands. She wished for Lily's comforting presence, but, of course, she would not be allowed to look on anything as terrible as this for fear her baby might be marked. Chewing her lips, Emma wondered if Harrison was avoiding her. He had brought her no word about Jonathan.

Sick in mind and body, Emma struggled to do what was expected of her. Cordelia insisted she go each day; however, when she was at Barbour Hall, her sister-in-law's demands upon her increased, and she was already weary when she reported for duty. One morning a dying man asked her to read the Bible to him.

"Read the Gospel of John," he rasped. "It's the easiest to understand and the most comforting."

Her own voice was becoming hoarse by the time she had read to the sixth chapter. "And when even was now come," she said softly, aware that men all about her had stopped their thrashing to listen, "his disciples went down unto the sea, and entered into a ship, and went over the sea toward

Capernaum. And it was now dark, and Jesus was not come to them."

Emma looked at the men, many of whom were seafarers, and continued, "And the sea arose by reason of a great wind that blew. So when they had rowed about five and twenty or thirty furlongs, they see Jesus walking on the sea, and drawing nigh unto the ship: and they were afraid."

She tried to moisten her mouth. "But he saith unto them, It is I; be not afraid. Then they willingly received him into the ship: and immediately the ship was at the land whither they went."

Around her, stillness remained. Suddenly, a man behind Emma began to shake. Quickly she covered the feverish man with all the blankets she could find.

"That chill like to shook me clean out of the garrison," he said through chattering teeth.

Dr. Weedon came to her side. "Many of these mariners have malaria from the miasmas emanating from stagnant water," he said. "We must have some of the quinine substitute. Miss Emma, please go and see if the bark has been collected."

Glad to escape, she turned away.

"And bring some carrots for poultices," Dr. Pope called after her.

When she returned, the boy had died. The older man who had the chill told her, "He went whispering, 'It is I; be not afraid.' "

Tears stung her eyes. She turned without a word and stumbled blindly to find Dr. Weedon.

Wearily he shook his head as he accepted what she had brought. "It's bad enough to try to treat wounds with herbs and bark instead of medicine," he sighed, "but worse, we can't get surgical instruments through the blockade. I'm amputating with a carpenter's saw. I've made a pair of retractors from the iron bale of a water bucket. I'm even reduced to using knitting needles and common table forks for surgical instruments." His briskness gone, he sat for a few moments, then stood, seeming to move each part of his body with a separate effort. "Mrs. Stow took sick. You'll have to help me. Come."

Emma knelt in bloody water, fighting nausea as a patient clutched her hand while Dr. Weedon cauterized a gangrenous sore and cut away black, dead tissue. He washed it out with whiskey and plugged the wound with raw cotton soaked in turpentine.

Dizzily, she dropped in a corner. Utterly exhausted, she hung down her head and fell into a doze. Seconds later she jerked awake.

Her wild eyes lighted on a smooth-cheeked boy. "Michael!" She knelt beside him and pushed damp hair from a thin face that could have seen no more than fifteen summers. Shaking with a chill, she realized this lad could almost have been her child. Teeth chattering with the impact of how many years had passed since she had seen Michael, she stumbled outside. Under the magnolia tree she wept. The evening of her life had come. A gnawing at her brain warned that she had lost Jonathan even as she had lost Michael. As this awful war was drawing to its bloody end, her life was drawing to a painful close.

She could not go back into the Tavern. Without seeing where she was going, she walked the long distance to Lily's house. In a trancelike state, she played with the joy-filled Mignonne, lifting a tiny, china cup to her lips in a pretend tea party.

At last, she lifted pain-filled eyes to Lily's lovely face and said in anguish, "I can't go on. I just can't stand it anymore! I'm not a Florence Nightingale."

"I wish I could relieve you awhile," said Lily. "But everyone refuses to let me take a turn. Perhaps you are wrong in thinking it was easy for Miss Nightingale. I've been reading more about her." Lily brought a book and placed it before Emma's unseeing eyes.

With the back of her hand pressed against her lips, the pale girl sat unmoving.

Frowning anxiously, Lily continued earnestly, "Miss Nightingale seemed a model of compassion, but she had no joy. It was not self-forgetting service, but the attainment of proud self-satisfaction. After her Crimean height, she wrote that her lamp showed her own utter shipwreck on the rock of self-willed pride in her devotion to duty. Only after years of bitterness did she pray for forgiveness and submit herself to God's outstretched hand."

Too exhausted to sleep, Emma tossed fitfully throughout the night. When she stepped into the Tavern yard next morning, she clapped her hand to her mouth in horror. There, awaiting disposal, strewn about like so much cordwood, lay several amputated limbs.

She ran.

Down the river she ran until she was totally alone. Flinging herself prostrate on the edge of the bluff, she vomited into the muddy red Chattahoochee. Her body wet with sweat in the hundred-degree heat, her heart beating rapidly, her emotions churning, pulling, tugging in every direction, she cried out to God. "Why, why, Lord, why?"

She rose shakily to her feet and thrust both fists heavenward. Wavering, nearly falling into the chasm of the summer-low water far, far below, she did not really care if she fell. Suddenly the wind began to whip her skirt, to snatch her hair from its confining knot. The rushing wind whirled round her, dipped down, and whipped the sleeping river into a choppy sea.

Lowering around her, the black sky suddenly split. The clap of thunder which followed the lightning's gash shook her to her knees. Huge drops of rain pelted her, merging with her tears.

"Dear Lord," she sobbed, "Lily says You care about every person. Do You really care about someone as worthless as I?" She looked up into the stormy sky, bursting as only July's intensity could explode.

"Forgive me, Lord. I know You created this world — and You created me as I am for some purpose. I've always known Jesus died for the sins of the world, but I didn't want to believe He died for my sins. I thought I had to earn a place in heaven. Was that what Lily meant about Miss Nightingale? Forgive me, Lord. Forgive me for hardening my heart against You!"

Suddenly, into her mind rushed the words

which had eased the young man's dying. The disciples had just been shown that Jesus is the Bread of Life; yet, they had headed their ship across the dark sea without Him. They were afraid.

Speaking clearly in her mind, a voice said, *"It is I; be not afraid!"*

Emma's breathing slowed. Her gurgling stomach quieted. Her clutching hands which had torn the old muslin at the neck of her dress lay still in her lap.

"Come into my heart and take control of my life, Lord Jesus. I cannot go on alone," she said aloud.

Sitting quietly as the sun came out again and dried her clothing, Emma felt warmed by an inner peace. Her tears ceased. Stretching, inhaling the storm-cleansed air, she looked upward into the glory of the firmament. The greatness of God, Creator of this splendor, yet Lover of her individual soul, filled her with overwhelming joy.

Again in her mind the voice of the Holy Spirit spoke clearly. *"Go, I have prepared you for the task of proclaiming My love to these young men, of making of their deaths a victory. You can do it in My strength, for lo, I am with you always, even unto the end of the world."*

An inner calm now matched her placid

smile. "Lead me, Lord," she prayed. Certain now of love and strength and purpose, she walked back into the hospital.

During her absence, a new load of patients had arrived. On a cot in a far corner lay Jonathan Ramsey.

CHAPTER 13

Blinking, trying to adjust her eyes to the dim light, Emma rubbed them. Perhaps the trick of vision, mind, and heart that had played upon her nerves a false Michael was tantalizing her again. Slowly she moved across the room. The hair on the dirty pillow curled black as a bird's wing; the brows etched a frown against skin which shone like wax in a slanting ray of sunlight. "Jonathan," she gasped, dropping to her knees beside him.

His eyelids fluttered. Weakly he raised a trembling hand to the damp, golden strands frizzling upon her forehead, glowing in the sunbeam. "Are you real?" he rasped. "Is that a halo? Are you an ang—"

"I'm real, oh, I'm real and here with you!" she cried, laughing, weeping, grasping the shaking hand and smothering kisses upon the back, the palm. She turned so that the light behind her would show him her face.

"Oh, Emma. I didn't want you to know!"

"Jonathan, I love you. Of course I must know. I love you." She clutched his hand to her cheek and washed it with her tears. Tenderness and love for him overwhelmed her. "I love you!" she repeated, not holding back merely because he did not speak the words to her. How desperately she had loved him, needed him to give her a sense of importance and self-esteem. Now, her love leaped from such narrow confines and enwrapped him, nurtured him. "My precious Jonathan, how long have you been this ill?"

"Since the shipwreck on Saint George Island," he mumbled. "My old wound reopened. The infection is in the bone, they say. The open sore has grown from one inch to three. I didn't want to come here." He pulled his hand from hers and dropped his arm over his eyes. "All they seem to know is amputation . . . I won't have that! I won't!"

"Sometimes it's necessary," she soothed, "the only thing to save a life. But there's other hope. Dr. Weedon makes a healing salve of alder pitch and blooms." She patted him and spoke with a confidence which belied what her eyes told her. "We'll soon have you well."

"How calm you are, how sweet," he

sighed. "I feel stronger already."

Happily, she bathed his face and hands and brought him water. She searched out Dr. Weedon and attended him as he treated Jonathan's greenish, running sore. When Jonathan fell into a peaceful sleep, her joy gave wings to her feet. Soul singing, she hurried to share the wonderful events with Lily.

Days followed swiftly as Emma ministered to Jonathan and the others with a new sense of purpose. With her focus no longer inward but upward, outward, she moved among them without her old, paralyzing fears that someone would whisper behind her back, or laugh at her, or worst of all, snub her. Often she needed to quote Lily's favorite verse, "I can do all things through Christ which strengtheneth me," to get through a gruesome ordeal. Reassured that she was no longer alone, constantly sustained by prayer, she read the Scriptures and brought peace to the dying.

With her head throbbing from the stuffy sickrooms, Emma left the Tavern one morning for a walk along the bluff. The air smelled clean from the reviving rain of the night before. The cool breeze roughened her arms into goose bumps. She paused to look below her at the green river.

Wearily, she let her gaze drift down the mighty Chattahoochee as it stretched forth to meet the glorious canopy of fresh-washed sky. She lifted the tired lines of her face into a smile. For a moment she freed her mind from care as she absorbed the beauty. The magnitude of God exhilarated her senses.

Breathing a thankful prayer for the greatness of the Creator, she felt her soul filling with His presence. "Thank You, God, for loving me and caring what I do, for giving me a purpose to share Thy love with others," she breathed.

Bong! Bong! Bong! A lone church bell sounded. How had she forgotten the Sabbath? She must hurry to make her patients comfortable before she slipped away to church. Great as was her sense of God's grandeur in the beauty of nature, she needed to be in His house to lift her voice in praise and worship. And, oh, how she needed the strengthening fellowship of Christian brethren.

Gaily, she began to sing the old hymn, "Brethren, We Have Met to Worship." She continued to hum the tune as she moved through the Tavern infirmary.

As she drove the pony and buggy up the hill toward the church, Emma reflected that the whole town of Eufaula, safely separated by the river from the scenes of battle, had become a hospital. She passed sheds, erected south from Broad Street, which overflowed with sick and wounded from the Army of Tennessee and the Army of Virginia. Emma shook her head ruefully. She knew that many a swooning belle had plumbed her inner strength and resolutely become a nurse.

Sunday evening, Dr. Pope called upon them at Barbour Hall. The handsome man's pleasant features dropped with exhaustion as he spoke ingratiatingly to them. "I know you ladies are sacrificing greatly," he said, pursing his prominent lips, "and I hate to ask another thing, but the courthouse and the O'Harro House Hotel can hold no more wounded. We're beginning to fill private homes. Miss Cordelia, could we —" He cleared his throat. "May we use Barbour Hall for convalescent cases?"

Indignantly, Cordelia drew herself up and puffed out her ample chest. "Common soldiers — with goodness knows what diseases in my home? Certainly not!" she declared emphatically.

"Think about it, Ma'am," Dr. Pope pleaded. "We need to get some of these patients away from the hospital gangrene lest they be reinfected. You've always been known to attend every church service and to render good works."

Pride inflated Cordelia's cheeks. "Thank you for your kind words, Doctor, but Emma and I are women alone. We have no gentlemen relatives with us."

"You have your servants and many lovely rooms. There will be no scandal in these sad times."

Cordelia Edwards shook her head doubtfully.

"You should do it, Mama," said Lily, entering from the parlor doorway. "Pray about it."

"I'll let you know, Dr. Pope." Cordelia stood haughtily, indicating that he should leave.

After the doctor's departure, Lily turned her liquid brown eyes upon her mother. "Mama," she began hesitantly, "you and I have never looked at things the same way. You believe that salvation comes through righteous living and doing good works." She paused and drew in her breath. "I believe we are saved by Jesus' death for our sins — not by what we do — except repenting and obeying. Then the good we do is a joyful giving to Him by loving others. If we love Him, we must do for the least of these brethren."

Emma smiled at her. "How long did I hear this with my ear before I opened my heart to His Spirit?"

Cordelia Edwards whirled angrily and left them without a word. After a long interval, they heard her coming back down the stairs. She reentered the parlor with tears in her eyes.

"You were wiser than I, Daughter," Mrs. Edwards said in a voice filled with humility. "I have asked forgiveness for my pride in what I did for God and thankfully accepted what He has done for me."

The three women embraced, sisters in Christ.

"Run now, Emma, and tell Dr. Pope to send his patients. Quick!" She caught herself and chuckled. "Please."

Because Mrs. Edwards's room on the west rear of the house was shady and cool, she had her massive bed moved out and cots set up for a dozen patients.

"I'm putting you in charge of convalescent cases," Dr. Weedon told Emma, piercing her with his gaze for a long moment. "I'm also releasing Jonathan Ramsey to you. Have no false hope!" He shook his head. "He needs amputation, but he refuses. Indeed, he's too weak to stand the shock. What you must do is build his strength, and then . . ." He shrugged and turned to his patients.

In the pleasant atmosphere of Barbour Hall, the disheartened men improved. Daily, Emma applied the alder pitch salve to Jonathan's wound and prayed. Mrs. Edwards and Kitty worked diligently to care for their charges. Cordelia suffered her own illness without her former grumpiness, and sat with the men for motherly chats. Old Aunt Dilsey grumbled about cooking for so many men, but she set the children searching for eggs and sang lustily over the cook pots as she concocted light fare for delicate stomachs. Emma moved about with a sweet smile and a look of deep contentment in her eyes.

She noticed that Jonathan's restlessness was assuaged when she played the piano in the long August evenings. Her fingers caressed the mother-of-pearl keys in the deliberate, soothing notes of Beethoven's Sonata Number 14, "Moonlight." With an eye to Jonathan's crutch, she avoided waltzes and played Chopin's romantic nocturnes. The music flowed like liquid silver through the candlelit house.

Sitting on the porch to catch the cooling evening breeze, Jonathan smiled sadly at her with longing in his eyes. "Seeing you bustling about domestic duties makes me dream that you are my wife and mistress of Magnolia Springs," he said wistfully. He reached for her hand and clutched it.

"That happy day will surely come soon," Emma replied with her eyes full of love. "For now I'll enjoy just being near you, seeing you get better day by day." Her accepting love held him gently. No longer thinking of herself at all, she relaxed and savored their private moment.

"How can you be so content?"

"God loves me; you love me; I have purpose in life," she laughed. Seeing his face cloud with misery, she drew back regretfully, knowing she had said the wrong thing.

"And I have none!" he flung out bitterly. "I sit here a cripple while the *Chattahoochee* is nearly ready to fight again."

"If she recovered, so can you! Even as a crippled ship, she had use keeping the enemy at bay."

"What use have I?" He raked his fingers through dark curls grown shaggy and unkempt.

Emma's pale blue eyes searched his face in the moonlight. Realizing how deeply depressed he had become, she said softly, "You're of great use to me. You couldn't know how lost and alone and desperate I'd become that day when you arrived at the

Tavern. Let me share . . ."

Tenderly, he took her face in both his hands and seemed calmed by her peacefulness. "Dear Emma. Lovely Emma," he whispered and kissed her lightly.

Jonathan tried valiantly, but fever drained him. He seemed to have forgotten all his funny stories, and he smiled only when Mignonne was there with her trilling laughter and unending chatter. The beautiful tot would run by him with her dark eyes flashing and her long brown curls bobbing, demanding that he grab at her and tease; then, she would plop her sturdy little body into his lap for a story. Lily brought her often. Although it was considered unseemly for anyone as great with child as Lily to be seen in public, she declared Barbour Hall was home; and she must be allowed to come and help with these recovering men.

One afternoon as Emma stepped onto the porch for a breath of air, she saw a handsome young man swinging across the yard as if he owned it. Lean, virile, vastly different from her lifeless charges, he bounded up the steps and smothered her in a hug.

"Foy!" she exclaimed joyfully as he lifted her in a whirling jig.

The family gathered around the table

while Foy ate. "The *Muscogee*," he told them, "is almost ready for launching!" Beneath heavy brows, his smoldering eyes met Jonathan's. "The iron supply's still low." He shoved in another spoonful. "She's been armored only at the knuckle, but six, seven-inch rifles from Catesby Jones's Naval Foundry at Selma are in place." He gulped buttermilk. "Officially she's been named the CSS *Jackson* after the Mississippi capital." He laughed. In a deep, resonant voice, he added, "But we'll always use the yard name, *Muscogee*."

Bringing all of the food that was left in the pie safe, Emma looked at the sun-bleached hair tousled around his ears and smiled. With a pang she realized he was now eighteen. *When did our flop-eared, owl-eyed little boy become a man?*

Foy's whirlwind visit increased Jonathan's longing to return to duty; however, his health did not improve. Dr. Weedon came, accompanied by Mary Young, whom he was now affectionately calling by her pet name, Molly. The doctor frowned and shook his head at Emma when he examined Jonathan's foot and drained the wound.

For diversion and relief from the heat of the stifling stillness of September, Emma hitched the runabout and took Jonathan to visit Fairview Cemetery, where his friends from the hospital rested in their graves.

Moving slowly on his cumbersome crutch, he walked with Emma to the grassy bank, where they stood looking down the cliff into Chewalla Creek, rushing to meet its destiny with the Chattahoochee.

Yearning to take Jonathan in her arms and kiss away his tears as she would Mignonne's, Emma looked at the defeated man with tender compassion and prayed for wisdom to help him.

"Jonathan," she began hesitantly as they sat down on the bank, "I was struggling so desperately until the voice of God spoke to me through the Scriptures as I was reading to the patients . . ."

He patted her hand absently, but his eyes roamed far down the flowing river.

"What helped me most," she continued shyly, "was the story of the disciples out on the stormy sea. They were helpless, afraid. Jesus came walking to them saying, 'It is I; be not afraid.' " Between Jonathan and Emma, the sultry air hung lifeless, still. Jonathan continued to stare unseeingly at the water. She took a deep breath and plunged on. "The minute they let Him into the boat, they were at the land where they were going. Let Jesus into your heart. It will help you through . . ."

He turned to her and lifted her hand to rub it against the stubble of his beard. "You're so sweet," he said sadly. "I accepted Christ and was baptized when I was ten. It was meaningful to me then. Bible stories are helpful for teaching a child and for easing a dying man. You're doing a good work, Emma." Reaching for his crutch, he struggled to his feet, shrugging off her help, dismissing her.

A week after its occurrence they heard the terrible news that on September 2, 1864, Sherman had captured Atlanta. Rumors abounded that he had begun a march to the sea.

Excitement leaped again on the twenty-second of December. Jonathan hobbled into the kitchen to find Emma. Whooping for joy, he shouted, "The *Muscogee*'s been launched! They say she glided into the water so smoothly that the motion wouldn't have shaken the water in a tumbler," he exulted. "Emma, send for Dr. Weedon. I must get back to duty! Even the *Columbus Daily Enquirer* calls our ironclad a crowning achievement. The Union is shaking in fear. They've increased the blockade, but our ram will break it."

Clutching her frayed cashmere shawl

about her shoulders as she started her search for Dr. Weedon, Emma realized that Jonathan did not know the strength of the blockade. No supplies were getting through. Christmas dinner was made up of make-dos, substitutions for the regular holiday fare. No eggs, no chicken — they were reserved for the very ill. The hogs had subsisted on what they could forage in the streets and were too thin to kill.

Worst of all, with no way to market cotton to bring in cash, Lily had sold her best Paris gowns to provide necessities. If she had had gold, there was nothing to buy for Mignonne. Tearfully the four year old was told that Santa Claus could not get through the blockade and must save his toys for next year.

Dr. Weedon drained Jonathan's foot again. He would not consent to the sick man's returning to the navy.

When Kitty and Tildy burst into her bedroom on Christmas morning with shouts of "Chris'mus gif'," Emma had nothing for them. She buried her head under the covers and cried.

Mignonne played happily with toy animals which Lily had fashioned from rags and chicken feathers, but the family's day was crowned with bitterness when the word passed around Eufaula that General W. T. Sherman had wired Abraham Lincoln, "I beg to present you as a Christmas gift the city of Savannah," after having taken the city on the twentieth of December.

New Year's Day, 1865, brought the delayed news that since September, Sherman had been marching through Georgia, ravaging a swath sixty miles wide across the state from Atlanta to the sea, and Magnolia Springs Plantation had fallen victim to his pillage. There was no word on the whereabouts of his family, but crops in the fields, barns, outbuildings — everything had been set ablaze. The beautiful house had been looted, torched. Nothing remained of the house but two blackened chimneys. Crushing the letter savagely, the disease-ridden man could not hold back his tears.

Emma could not bear to watch him. Disconsolately, she laid her head upon his knee.

"All that's left are Mother's rubies," Jonathan said at last. "I'm so glad I sent for them." His voice seemed to be coming from a great distance. Idly, he plucked at her hair. "They are yours. Keep them. I release you from your vow. I cannot marry you now!"

"No, Jonathan, no." She lifted her head aghast and looked at him wild-eyed. "I've never had worldly goods. It doesn't matter to me that you have no fine house to take me to." She grasped out to embrace him. "All I want is to be your wife!"

"You've lived in luxury," he replied curtly, drawing away from her reaching hands.

"As a servant. Until now. Cordelia treats me like a sister lately." Her aching, empty arms hugged about her own shoulders.

"Yes." His voice sounded harsh, hollow. "I've noticed the change in her. She'll take care of you. I cannot marry you with nothing!" He hobbled away.

Like winter's unrelenting cold, Jonathan's impersonal gaze froze Emma in its icy grip. Even the joy of Lily's delivery of Harrison Wingate, Jr., on February 22, 1865, was diminished because his father was not at home. Somberly, Emma stood over Lily, reflecting that an eon ago, before the war when Mignonne was born, she had been sent away from the house because she was a maiden lady. *Now I'm a nurse,* she thought.

Panting, sweating, gripping Emma's hand, Lily cried, "Oh, I wish Harrison was here!" She tried to laugh. "In times like this I wish Mama had been right when she used to tell me you found babies out in the cabbage patch!"

Emma smiled halfheartedly. She, too,

wished for the security the quiet man's presence always gave, but he was on a downriver expedition on the *William H. Young*. The threats of a few such steamers and the *Chattahoochee* and *Muscogee* still held the river safe.

But the enemy advanced from the west.

General James H. Wilson's cavalry galloped through Alabama like a spring tornado. Captain Catesby Jones's Selma Naval Foundry was his first target. The niter works, the powder mill and magazine, the whole industrial town of Selma which was forging half the Confederacy's cannon, making two-thirds of the fixed ammunition, exploded and burned with sulfurous black smoke like Dante's *Inferno*.

Bugles blaring, Wilson's troopers charged down upon Montgomery, torched eighty-five thousand bales of cotton worth forty million dollars, threw sixty thousand bushels of corn into the flames, rode on through the pall of smoke, and stopped short at the banks of the Chattahoochee River swollen by spring rains, swirling at flood stage.

With shaking hands, Eufaulians read reports in April 14's *Columbus Daily Sun* and murmured encouragement to each other because the newspaper stated, "Everything is in readiness for battle. Let us keep calm." Unsure of Foy's whereabouts, the women of Barbour Hall remained on their knees in prayer as reports filtered through of two brigades moving up to attack Columbus.

Breathlessly, the city waited. Bulging with refugees from Alabama, fleeing Wilson, and from Georgia, fleeing Sherman, the river city trembled with only old men, boys, and walking wounded to protect her. Georgia's General Howell Cobb rushed in, but he had only two thousand unseasoned troops to guard the bridges. Frantically, the Confederates rendered the northernmost bridge unusable, tore up plank flooring of the southernmost, Dillingham Street Bridge, and settled into two forts at the Fourteenth Street Bridge. With four, ten-pound Parrots bearing on the road, they waited.

Wilson swept through Girade, Alabama, and massed for attack. Surprisingly, the bugles blew "Water Call." As the Bluecoats tended their horses and rested, Columbus waited. On the morning of April 16, Columbus prepared. At two in the afternoon, Yankee troopers were visible on the hills. Confederate batteries shelled ineffectually. No answering fire came. They waited.

Night descended, clear, moonless. At eight o'clock, the still, quiet blackness as of midnight was shattered by a shot, another, ten thousand more. Flashes puncturing the dark shroud pinpointed Confederate strong points.

Yelling, "Selma, Selma, go for the bridge!" Union troops charged.

In chaos of darkness, men fought, struggled on the bridge, confused friend with foe in the utter blackness of the covered wooden span. The smell of turpentine flared nostrils. A Confederate match was struck, shot down. At eleven o'clock, General Wilson rode into Columbus.

Panic ensued. Women and children ran through the streets. The confused sounds of flight rumbled through a night suddenly bright as midday. One hundred thousand bales of cotton bloomed at midnight in a fiery blaze. For miles the earth trembled as explosions rocked the arsenal, the Naval Ironworks, Haiman and Brother Sword Factory. Vowing to destroy everything, Wilson wrecked the railroad and burned the quartermaster depot.

Capturing the *Jackson/Muscogee,* the Union troops set fire to the vessel, cutting her adrift. The formidable ram careened down the Chattahoochee and sank on a shoal with her armor melted.

By the end of the seventeenth, Columbus

lay in ashes. The paper mill, the flour mill, the Eagle Textile Mill, the bridges — everything was burned. The *Daily Sun* and the *Columbus Times* were wrecked. The *Memphis Appeal* which had fled from city to city ended its wandering publication. Only the *Daily Enquirer*'s presses remained intact, but Wilson forced the paper to cease publication.

No further word reached Eufaula. At Barbour Hall, no message came from Foy.

Then one morning a rumpled, disheveled young man with singed hair and eyebrows walked stiffly across the yard. "I lit the match to the *Chattahoochee.*" Foy grinned ruefully.

"No!" his family chorused. "What happened?"

"It was the first time I ever saw shelling at night." He sat with arms hanging limply. "A beautiful but awful spectacle. Every second our eyes were blinded by the blue light of shells exploding around us. Grape and canister came whistling by." He shook his head sorrowfully and rubbed the stub of his eyebrows.

"Wilson's raiders captured the *Muscogee,* stripped her, set her burning." He nodded at Jonathan, knowing how proud he had been of the *Chattahoochee.* "We couldn't let 'em ravish our lady. We escaped as far as Race Pass. There was nothing else to do." He swallowed bitterness. "Our crew wet her decks with kerosene, ignited slow fuses, and retreated by the firelight." He dropped his head in his hands.

Jonathan lay on his cot submerged in despair. Hatred of Sherman and Wilson and the unnecessary devastation they had wreaked poisoned his soul even as his wounded foot poisoned his blood. Again and again he went over the awful story with Foy, lamenting, cursing the destruction that had taken place a week after General Robert E. Lee's surrender to General U. S. Grant, April 9, 1865. It made him feel no better that Wilson, coming in from the west, had known neither of the armistice nor of the fact that on April 14, the Stars and Stripes were raised over Fort Sumter; and on that night Lincoln had been shot.

Except for a few last skirmishes in the west, the April 16 battle for Columbus was the last. The long, agonizing War Between the States was over.

Emma gave Jonathan all her loving care, praying for him constantly and asking Lily's and Cordelia's prayers, too. He had lost the will to live; she tried to resign herself to the fact that he was dying.

Emma felt she had to get away, if only for a moment, to escape the sick, the dying. Not wanting even Kitty with her, she hitched the runabout and drove out the road west of Eufaula. Flexing her shoulders in the warm morning sun and inhaling the fragrance of honeysuckle, she found it hard to believe that her favorite month, April, had passed in such a blur, but, yes, it was the twenty-eighth day. Beneath the dark pines, sparkling white dogwood turned the woodland into a fairyland. She tried to let the beauty lighten her spirits, but something was missing. There was no music. At first she thought that melody was merely absent from her soul, but as she began to look around uneasily, she realized that the birds had hushed their singing. No squirrels played along the ground.

Slapping the reins, she urged the pony toward Oak Hill Plantation. She entered the gates with a sigh of relief.

Her friend, Matilda, greeted her delightedly. Gray had streaked her hair since word came that her husband had died at Seven Pines, but her face, still young, wreathed in smiles as she poured tea made of rose hips

265

and other odd, unsatisfying ingredients. They settled down to chat.

Galloping horses pounded into the yard. Sloshing their tea, Emma and Matilda rushed to the open door as a bluecoat officer stamped onto the porch with a clanking of spurs.

"Set food out," he demanded in an accent harsh to their ears. "My men are hungry."

Matilda looked around her yard at the dozen men. "We can give you a little bread, but that's all we have," she said with her head held high. She turned and nodded at a trembling servant.

The man glowered at her and snorted.

A sudden realization flooded over Emma that these men, like Wilson, might have been beyond communication. She quickly stepped forward. "The armistice has been signed," she said, proud of her firm voice. "You can do us no harm. The war is over!"

"We've not heard of an armistice," he replied curtly.

"Lee surrendered to Grant. Johnston to Sherman. Lincoln's dead!" Then she repeated firmly. "You dare not harm us."

He recoiled in shock. Grimacing, he took off his forage cap and scratched red hair. Eyeing her suspiciously, he snarled, "You might be telling the truth — but Lincoln dead?" He dropped his hand to the Colt pistol in his belt. "No! No such message has reached us. We've received no parcel of change of orders. We're advance guard. Must hurry on. If — if it's true —" he threw them another puzzled look and shrugged — "I can afford you no protection. The command will soon be passing."

Taking the food Matilda proffered, he clanked down the steps. Greedily eating cold cornbread, the men whirled their horses out of the yard. Breaking branches off the trees, they threw them on the ground to guide the advancing army.

"Quickly, quickly." Matilda clapped her hands and directed her frightened household. "Bar the doors!"

Emma reached outside the windows, closed the green shutters, and fastened them. Matilda worked swiftly behind her removing the sticks and lowering the glass. With everything as secure as possible, they stood peering through the cracks in the wooden shutters, waiting.

A lone figure struggled up the lane. Recognizing the white-haired lady in faded silk as their neighbor, Matilda threw off the bars, and they hurried to meet her just as her knees buckled.

"I escaped — across — the fields," she

panted. "They burned my house. Destroyed everything!"

With the younger women on each side half-dragging her, they moved slowly toward the porch. Looking around frantically, they lifted, pushed her inside, rebarred the door. Waited.

They heard them coming from afar, the unmistakable tread of marching men. Like a mighty, rushing water, the sound grew, pouring over them with drenching sweat. For an hour there was no break in the lines. They passed, a steady, solid stream of blue-coats, tramping by, leading weary, sore-footed horses.

Silently the women peered between the cracks, praying the army would march on without molesting them. Suddenly a sharp command was given. Mounted cavalrymen whirled into the yard, drew rein, turned carbines fixed with sabers upon the house. In the soft spring sunshine, they presented an unbroken line of glittering steel.

A pounding on the heavy front door and a shout, "Open!" echoed through the house. Mutely, the women shrank back. *Crash!* The ruby glass of the sidelight shattered against their skirts. Through the gash, the ugly nose of the Spencer carbine brandished its wicked bayonet.

"Ahhh!" Matilda clapped her hand over her mouth to stifle her scream.

Emma leaned close to the jagged hole and shouted, "Stop that at once. There's been an armistice. We will not open the doors. You dare not break them down. Lee surrendered to Grant! The war is over!"

Cursing, threatening to torch the house with them in it, the Yankee demanded they open the door.

"We will not!" She looked around at the women and children. "Your advance guard took all we had." Mustering all of the authority into her voice that she could, she shouted the information she had given the guard and ended with a command. "The hostilities have ceased. You dare not harm us or burn this house!"

For an endless moment, all was silent. Emma stole a quick look through the sidelight. The huge man stood deliberating. He reached into the paraphernalia banded across his body and brought out a twist of tobacco as long as his hand. He chomped into the horrid brown stuff and gnawed off a cheekful. Chewing thoughtfully, he turned and stalked off with the metal scabbard of his low-slung saber dragging, scraping the floor, leaving an indelible scar. He stopped to bark at his men. He turned back. Emma shrank fearfully from her peephole.

Hesitating curses, shuffling feet, clapping, clanking arms, told her they were leaving the porch. Exhaling at last, she dissolved to the floor in a pool of sweat.

With tears streaming down their cheeks, the women ran from room to room, peering through the cracks in the shutters and watching the hams and bacon taken from the smokehouse, the dairy house emptied, the stock turned from the barn, and the corn cribs dumped. Doors were wrenched from their hinges, gates kicked down. And all the while the detachment wreaked their devastation, the column of the army trod relentlessly down the road.

For two hours they passed. Dusk gathered before the enemy was out of sight and all was silent again.

"I must get home." Emma's flat, determined voice startled them as she broke the silence.

"No, Emma, it's too dangerous!" shrieked Matilda.

"I must warn them. The bluecoats are headed for Eufaula. They'll burn our beautiful town. I told you what they did to Columbus. Foy said some of the soldiers even took the ladies' dresses and made feed bags for their horses."

Matilda stood openmouthed, soundless with horror.

Emma looked at the exhausted old woman behind them and the crying children pulling at Matilida's skirts. "I hate to leave you," she told her friend, "but there's only a handful of old men and boys with all those women and wounded. No one to stop them before they come in shooting and burn the town. I must warn them. I must!"

They were afraid to open the door. Tiptoeing into the yard, they found the small runabout, its silver mountings missing; the red cushions, slashed. The pony was nowhere to be seen. Matilda's horse and carriage were gone.

"You can't walk!"

"I'm not a good rider anyway." Emma laughed shakily. "I'll have to go cattycornered through the woods to head them off."

Hugging Matilda, she started resolutely across the rough ridges of a plowed field. Fearful that more soldiers might be coming down the road, she glanced behind her, stumbled, fell flat. With her breath knocked out of her, she lay condemning herself for stupidity. Hearing a noise, she clambered on hands and knees without looking back until she reached the dark safety of the

271

woods. Snatching her skirt free from the blackberry briars which ringed the field, she lunged into the thick forest.

Stepping carefully now, she tried desperately to concentrate on direction, to avoid the grasping arms of vines, to watch for snakes, to listen. . . . Jingling reins and whinnying horses told her she had strayed too far north toward the road. She stopped, pressing herself flat against an oak. The cavalry was mounted now; rested horses trotted faster toward Eufaula.

Exhausted, her feet aching from paper-lined shoes, she huddled behind the tree until sound ceased. Wearily, she dragged to her feet and hurried on. Running, walking, hobbling, frantic now, she feared she would lose her way as darkness leaped before her, thwarting her like a big black gnome.

Catching her foot on a log, she fell and began to cry. She thought of the tales of Wilson's march — how he had left the road from Selma through Montgomery black with the smoke of burning mansions and putrid with the stench of dead horses and mules. Women had been made to give up their jewels, and trusted servants had been threatened with death if they did not help to burn and destroy.

Emma had confused one soldier briefly,

but when the officers arrived they would destroy without asking. *Beautiful Eufaula,* she wept, *where Lily and Mignonne waited alone without Harrison, where only Cordelia tended Jonathan and the wounded.* "Jonathan," she sobbed. Struggling to her feet, she pressed onward, praying for strength.

At last, she came out of the forest and stood at the top of the hill looking down upon Eufaula, candlelit, peaceful. With her last strength, she hurried to Dr. Pope's house on Broad Street. But Dr. Pope, Eufaula's mayor, was not there. Staring in amazement at Emma's torn, dirty clothing and scratched face and hands, Mrs. Pope listened to her tale. Helping Emma into her buggy, she whipped the horse and raced toward the Tavern.

Patting Emma as she talked, the doctor pursed his lips and nodded absently at the details, which poured from her lips as though unbidden. Finally, he stopped her story and began snapping orders. Able-bodied men were few. The townsmen had not yet returned home from fields of battle. He sent two teenaged boys, Edward Young and Edward Stern, galloping westward waving a white flag of truce.

Emma sank gratefully upon her bed while her warning passed around the town like leaping flames. Frantically the women buried their silver in their gardens, and hid their precious sugar and flour between the ceilings and roofs of their houses.

At dawn on the twenty-ninth of April, the youthful couriers galloped back into town. Shrugging that they had not found the enemy encampment, they innocently explained that they had stopped at a house and spent the night. Exasperated, Dr. Pope sent them out again down the Clayton Road to present the white flag and delay the attack while he gathered the prominent, older men who were city councilmen to go with him to face the enemy.

Emma had rested only a few hours when a small boy brought a cryptic note from Dr. Pope.

Dress in your Sunday best. Go at once to my house. We have a plan to save the town. I'm relying upon you.

C. J. Pope

Puzzled, she washed her face and put on her best pink taffeta frock. She had not worn the rubies since that unspeakable day when Jonathan had said he could not marry her. For some defiant, unfathomable reason, she put on the necklace and the large ruby ring. Carefully she arranged her hair. She fastened the green shutters, barred the doors, and hurried out into the silent streets.

When she reached the house at the foot of the hill on the north side of Broad Street, she found Mrs. Pope, bustling about, preparing a fine meal. "Here, Emma, set the table with my finest china and silver." Mrs. Pope laughed ironically. "It makes my Southern blood boil to have to serve them." She wiped a wisp of gray hair from her damp forehead and shrugged. "But Dr. Pope insists that this is the only way to save us from the torch. We must entertain them like gentlemen and keep them occupied until they can receive their orders to prove the war is over."

All morning, the ladies of the town helped Mrs. Pope and her daughter, Ella, not daring to think what would happen if the plan failed.

Just before noon, they heard the sound, the rattle of sabers, the jingling of reins, the clopping hoofs of hundreds upon hundreds of horses. The regiment crested the hill, the muffled drumbeat livened, was joined by fifes, and the jaunty tune, "Yankee Doodle," echoed through the streets.

Emma clapped her hands to her buzzing ears. She shook her head, unsure, but, yes, she heard the plaintive notes of a violin. A frightened moan escaped her lips as she saw Professor J. C. Van Houten across the street on the steps of Miss Sarah Shorter Hunter's house. The blind musician had tucked his violin beneath his chin. How could he be so defiant? He was playing "Dixie."

The band blared the louder as it passed. Next came the entourage, Dr. Pope and the councilmen escorting the gold-braided officers into the yard and onto the porch. Emma retreated behind the lace curtains to watch as the officers in alien blue deposited part of their weapons on the porch.

The majestic man with epaulets must be the general. While some of the men swaggered with the four-foot scabbards slung from their left hips and dragging the ground, he walked smartly with his saber carefully fastened up with a hook. Lean, hard-muscled, he wore a short blue jacket resplendent with brass buttons and, tucked into knee-high boots, light blue trousers with a yellow stripe down the leg. With dignity, he handed over his saber and holstered pistol to his guard. As he carefully folded his gauntlets into his wide leather belt, Emma knew the moment had come.

Pressing her fingertips against her stiff cheeks, she put on a pleasant smile as she stepped into the entrance hall. The tall man removed his slouch hat and gave a slight bow as she and the other women swished forward. Hope rose that he was a gentleman.

"Ladies, may I present Brevet Major-General Benjamin H. Grierson," said Dr. Pope with false heartiness.

Acknowledging him with a gracious nod, Emma was startled at the appraising look he swept over her. Just then the strains of "Dixie" emanated so strongly from across the street that she feared he would become angry. Scarcely knowing what she said, she greeted the general with chattering charm as Lily would have done. The tall man smiled down at her sardonically.

Dr. Pope explained that he had directed General Grierson to send his men across the Chattahoochee River to Harrison's Mill near Georgetown, Georgia, where a spring would provide water for their camp.

Mrs. Pope welcomed the officers to her table, pitching her voice higher than usual against the unending sounds of clopping hoofs, jingling reins, and marching feet in horrifying counterpoint to the spirited mingled rhythms of "Yankee Doodle" and "Dixie." Using all her ingenuity to stretch her meager supply of food, she served many courses. Over after-dinner coffee, made of roasted grain, she tactfully pointed out to the general the heartbreaking conditions in the South brought about by the war. Then she invited the satiated men into the music room.

Against the discordant noise outside, Emma played several selections on the piano. John McNab's little daughter was brought in to sing. General Grierson, who had said little but had conducted himself like a gentleman, lifted the child to his knee and asked for a kiss.

"No, Sir." The little girl shook her head. She kicked his slick, black boot. "I won't kiss a Yankee!"

Emma's hand fluttered toward her chest, but then she stretched them toward Grierson placatingly. "Please excuse her, Sir." She laughed lightly. "She's just a child."

The general smiled with the lower half of his face only, set the tot down, and winked at Emma.

She held her breath fearfully as he gazed at her. What would he do? It was readily apparent that young and old of Eufaula would bend but not bow their spirits to their conquerors.

Suddenly he roared with laughter. "It seems I'm not the only one who doesn't know that the war has ended!" He stood up, obviously ready to leave. "I'll take your word." He nodded. "I'll accept your hospitality. I'll keep my men in camp and allow no foraging of the town until I receive my parcel with orders from General Sherman."

For twelve long hours, one company after another of men and horses appeared at the top of Broad Street and continued down upon them in a slow, tired march until four thousand cavalry had passed. Only when the last bluecoat had disappeared into the shadows of the covered wooden bridge spanning the Chattahoochee and stepped out of his adopted state, did the old man from New Jersey stop sawing the sad notes of "Dixie" and lay down his violin.

Exhausted, her nerves jangled, Emma dragged wearily back to Barbour Hall. Finally awakening Lige, who was guarding the door, she tiptoed in and lit a candle to check on the wounded men before she went to bed. Jonathan was not on his cot. Searching the huge house with rising fear, she fought far worse panic than the enemy had caused.

Jonathan was gone.

CHAPTER 14

"Jonathan!" she called out softly.

The flame from her candle etched eerie shadows against the walls, spider-webbed the high ceilings as she tiptoed from room to room, searching. He was not in the house. The belvedere? Surely not. The stairs would be painfully impossible, unless . . . She could not bear the thought that he might jump. Perhaps he had heard she was entertaining the Yankee general. Her knees jelly, she climbed the endless flights. He was not there.

Stumbling back down the passageways, she ran out into the yard. "Jonathan! Jonathan!" she called. Through the paths and gates and enclosures of the gardens, she searched. Empty. She peered fearfully up and down the deserted street. Leaves rustled behind her. Whirling, she glimpsed a night predator scurrying away. Letting out her breath, she realized she must not venture into the dark streets. The occupying army was everywhere, everywhere.

She could barely stand. Creeping to her bed, she lay with exhausted tears slipping out, soaking the pillow. Sleep came in snatches as she listened throughout the night for a sound to indicate that Jonathan had returned. She feared this final indignity of the conquering army had been more than he could bear. Since the Yankees had burned his plantation, he had slipped into a far place in his soul from which she could not lift him. He had lost the will to live.

As dawn streaked the sky, Emma rubbed swollen eyes and saw with surprise that she still wore her best pink taffeta. No matter now. She slid down from the high bed and hurried through the half-light to the stable. Cordelia's horse and carriage were gone. Whether they had been taken by Jonathan or by the invaders, she could not know. She stood with her hand trembling on the gate. Her eyes darted about, straining to see if anyone hid behind trees, around corners.

Seeing no one, she ran down the hill toward the river. Panting, she stepped into the dimly lit Tavern.

"Well, Emma, you're just in time." Dr. Pope looked up absently. "I'm in need of a dedicated nurse."

"No, Doctor, I — I can't stay — now." She labored for breath. "I'm looking for Jonathan Ramsey." She pushed back stray wisps of golden curls which were clinging to her damp forehead. "I thought maybe — is he here?"

"Um." He pursed his lips. "No. Haven't seen him." He shook his head. "Wait, Emma," he called out as she turned away. "Thank you for being such a great help yesterday. The Yankee, Grierson, was quite taken with you."

Emma nodded mutely, turned, and fled the Tavern, recoiling in horror as she saw bluecoat soldiers with axes raised. Crashing down, the axes split the heads of wooden barrels. Whiskey, which had been carefully hoarded for medicinal use, might now cause drunken rioting. Amber liquid gushed from the broken barrels and poured in streams into the ditch at her feet. Shoving her aside, men fell to their knees and lapped the whiskey from the ditch. Stumbling backward over a razor-backed hog, she sprawled in an undignified heap. Squealing, the hog pushed from under her hoop skirt. A herd of oinking pigs rooted between the men guzzling liquor. The pigs swilled until they staggered away as drunk as the men.

Stunned, Emma sat amazed. Suddenly she

began to laugh hysterically. Tears streaming, she struggled to her feet and stumbled to a secluded spot on the riverbank. As she looked down into the mists of morning, her breathing slowed, her hiccupping ceased. The wind, chilled from the long night, made the tear trails on her cheeks as icy as the fear made her heart.

Lifting her face into the wind, she prayed, "Strengthen me, O Lord. Help me to bear whatever comes. Help me not to waver from serving You." Then she began to sob. "Please, help me find Jonathan before it's too late."

Fairview Cemetery. The thought popped into her mind. He had gone there frequently of late to sit by the graves of his friends.

Walking, trotting, tripping, wondering if her lungs would burst and her feet in their worn, kidskin shoes would bleed before she covered another mile, she doggedly pressed onward.

There was no mistaking Cordelia's carriage. The horse was tethered by the graves of Confederate dead. The lemon-green lace of a weeping willow shivered around her. The slender branches danced frenziedly, whipped by a stiff breeze. She looked through a mist of tears and focused her eyes upon him at last. He was standing on the brink of the cliff.

Slowly, quietly, lest her sudden appearance startle him and make him jump, she crept forward.

Jonathan turned, raked his fingers through his black hair, looked at her blankly for a moment; and then he smiled. Slowly, as from a great depth, the smile spread over his face and lighted his eyes. As if from a century ago, she looked again into the eyes she loved, the dark and laughing eyes of Jonathan Ramsey.

He stretched out his arms. "Emma, my darling, you're always near when I need you. I love you. Oh, how I love you!"

Laughing, crying, not waiting to wonder why at last he said the words she had longed to hear, she flung herself into the haven of his embrace.

Kissing her hungrily, he stroked her flying hair and murmured again, "I love you."

A red ball of sun peeped from behind the dark green trees on the opposite shore. The tranquil black mirror of the Chattahoochee dazzled their tear-filled eyes with sparkling pinks and golds. Emma gazed wonderingly into his radiant face. He laughed and stopped her questioning with a smothering, passionate kiss which dizzied her, burning away the last mists of fear. Golden-green with new life, the trees around them housed orchestras of awakening birds. Melodies filled the April breeze. She leaned back at last, begged air, and looked into his dear face. Reaching up, she squeezed his curls and pushed back the lock from his forehead. Suddenly her knees gave way from her long searching and she swayed. Jonathan smoothed a place, and they sat on the grass beneath the sheltering arms of a blossoming dogwood.

Clasping the ruby on her hand, Jonathan smiled. "You never gave up on me, did you?" He fingered the heavy necklace, stroked her tender throat, and tilted her face for a gentle kiss. Looking at her adoringly, he said, "I must tell you — I know you've been praying for me, and I read the Bible where you marked it and left it by my cot." He paused, plucked a dogwood blossom from above their heads, and traced a thoughtful finger over the rusty holes in the cross the white flower formed around a crown of thorns. He cleared his throat. "I told you I accepted that Jesus died on the cross for my sins when I was a child. Unfortunately, when I reached my teens, I fell into what I thought were good times. As an adult, material possessions became my god."

He pulled her close. Peacefully, she nestled

her head on his shoulder. He kissed the golden curls on her forehead before continuing huskily. "God continued to bless me, but I worshiped money. My pride was my beautiful wife, my home. When she died —" He shook his head sorrowfully. "I turned to humanism, indulging myself. Even though I was yearning for spiritual things, I couldn't possess them. My soul was panting, but it couldn't rest. I was seeking but never finding, journeying yet never arriving . . ." His voice choked.

Gently Emma lifted her head and kissed his cheek. Happily, she knew that she could share her innermost thoughts with him, her spiritual depths, but for now she would sit quietly and let him talk.

"When I met you," he continued, "I blamed God for my problems. I couldn't love Him or myself — and much as I wanted to, I was afraid to love you. Afraid I'd lose you as I did Betty." He caught the hand which stroked his chin and kissed the palm. "Threatened with the loss of my foot — knowing you had to face the invaders alone — I was ready to throw myself into the Chattahoochee."

"What happened?" she whispered in awe.

"Your prayers, the dogwood, the message of Easter. Jesus suffered more than I. He arose. He lives! Suddenly I remembered that God is more powerful than all the evil in the world. I turned my whole life over to Him. I bowed before Him as my Lord." The weary lines of his face had vanished. His smile radiated his whole being. "You were right. The moment I let Jesus into the ship of my life I was at the land whither I went!"

The sun rose above the clouds, and morning burst brilliantly around them. Restlessness and searching ended, Emma sighed with deep contentment and tranquilly nestled against his shoulder. "I know now that God has a purpose for our lives," she said blissfully, "and that He will be with us and never let us bear our burdens alone."

"Yes," he answered quietly. "I'm not quite sure just yet what He wants me to do. Perhaps it's to share this message with others. It won't be easy. Our whole world is collapsing. I don't know what tomorrow will bring, but we'll trust God to provide our needs. With you and our children at my side, I can face each day rejoicing in doing God's will."

The smell of freshly turned earth was strong on the wind along the river as it caressed their joyful faces with the promise of a new beginning.

ACKNOWLEDGMENTS

Truth, it has been said, is stranger than fiction. Many events in this book would not be believable were they not true. The background characters were the heroes of the day. *The Wind Along the River* begins where *The River Between* left off and chronicles life in Eufaula, Alabama, during the Civil War and actual struggles for control of the Chattahoochee River. Only the center-stage figures who people Barbour Hall are fiction. The house itself is suggested by Fendall Hall, built in 1854 by Edward Young. Presently owned by the State of Alabama, it is open to the public.

Again, my appreciation goes to Douglas Purcell, Director of the Historic Chattahoochee Commission. His superb fund of knowledge guided me at every turning. Emma (Mrs. James Ross) Foy transported me back in time with innumerable small details. She, Jane Dempsey, and Hilda

289

Sexton of the Eufaula Heritage Association (located in Shorter mansion and open to the public) transcribed the diaries of Elizabeth Rhodes, which not only gave me the chronology of the events but the minds of those who experienced them.

The Confederate Navy came alive through the enthusiasm of Bob Holcombe, curator of the Confederate Naval Museum in Columbus, Georgia. There one can see the remains of the gunboat, *Chattahoochee,* and the ram, *Muscogee,* which were raised from their watery graves one hundred years later in 1965. Holcombe graciously schooled me in nautical matters and provided numerous references.

The recognized authority on the naval war on the local scene is Dr. Maxine Turner. She was very helpful to me, and her book, *Naval Operations on the Apalachicola and Chattahoochee,* became my guide

The love letters of George and Ellen Gift, collected in *Hope Bids Me Onward,* provided details of life aboard the *Chattahoochee* and the fact that ladies were often on the boats. Sarah Jones's journal, *Life in the South,* gave colorful details as did Bradlee's *Blockade Running.* Kane's *Christmas in the South* added validity to my knowledge of local customs, many of which remain to the present. Countless old books about the Confederate Navy and about medical problems of the era gave a sentence here and there.

My thanks goes to Harriet Bates of the Lake Blackshear Regional Library for securing books from all over the Southeast. One day when we had cross-checked a contradictory fact for the umpteenth time, I said, "My readers will skim over this without ever realizing the trouble we've taken to be accurate." She replied, "But aren't we having fun?"

Dr. Robert A. Collins assisted with medical matters, and the Reverend James D. Eldridge was helpful with the spiritual side. The music of the "Tallahassee Waltz" was unearthed in the Florida Collection of the State Library of Florida by librarian Linda Gail Brown. Thanks also go to Carolyn Nicholson, Marvlyn Story, and Glenda Spradley.

Eufaula, Alabama, was spared from the invader's torch just as I have described it from old memoirs. Especially poignant were *"Other Day's: A Transcript on Vellum"* by Anne Kendrick Walker and Mattie Thomas Thompson's *History of Barbour County, Alabama.*

Jacquelyn Cook

ABOUT THE SETTING OF
THE WIND ALONG THE RIVER

Southern hospitality at its finest awaits you at the annual Eufaula Pilgrimage in Eufaula, Alabama each year on the first weekend in April (unless Easter intervenes). Belles in hoop skirts stroll amid colorful azaleas and snowy dogwoods as you tour Greek Revival cottages and Italianate showplaces. These private residences are open for the occasion, and more hoop-skirted ladies await inside to tell you about the history of the homes and the antique furnishings. An art exhibit, gardens, afternoon teas, candlelight tours, and musical entertainment also delight visitors.

Alabama's oldest tour of homes, the Eufaula Pilgrimage was conceived in 1965 when the Eufaula Heritage Association was formed to buy Shorter Mansion as its headquarters. Built in 1884 by Eli Sims Shorter II and his wife Wileyna Lamar, it received extensive renovation in 1901-1906 that transformed it into the outstanding Greek Revival Mansion it is today. The House museum and cultural center is open to the public.

Learn more about Eufaula here: www.eufaulapilgrimage.com

ABOUT THE AUTHOR

Although **Jacquelyn Cook** has been a nationally published writer since 1963, selling over 500,000 copies of her first thirteen books, she considers herself first and foremost a southern author.

"My goal has been to write timeless stories of lasting values," says Cook. "I want to preserve our culture and history and the beauty of our landscape, but most of all I like to reflect the southerner's love of God, country, family and fellowman."

After gaining experience in journalism, Cook started writing the five-book *River* series that began with *The River Between,* published in 1985. After twenty–five years, these books are still in demand. In 2002, Barbour Books combined four of the popular stories in one volume called *Magnolias,* making it the complete novel Jacquelyn desired. Now, in 2010, BelleBooks is publishing beautiful new editions of the River series.

Wanting to write a longer, more fully developed novel, Cook began a new phase of her career with *Sunrise,* which was released in February 2008 by BelleBooks. Set in Macon, it is the fictionalized account of the true story of Anne Tracy and William Butler Johnston, who built the fabulous Johnston-Felton-Hay house in Macon, Georgia. Cook's extensive research was enhanced by family reminiscence of the Johnston's great-grandson George Felton. These personal materials made the story come alive.

Jacquelyn Cook has early ties to Macon because she majored in voice at Wesleyan Conservatory in the original building on College Street. "Memories of my days there have colored several of my books," she says.

An epic novel of the Civil War, *The Gates of Trevalyan,* followed in September 2008. The story of the King family on Trevalyan Plantation weaves into the tapestry of the most compelling historical figures of the time. Three love stories and exciting action keep pages turning.

The Greenwood Legacy, the true story of an amazing family who began the plantation culture that still exists in Thomasville,

Georgia, was released in 2009. It has delighted all who have read this novel of faith, family, love, and courage.

Mrs. Cook's family enjoys life on the ancestral farm near Lake Blackshear in Southwest Georgia. Jacquelyn's hobby is keeping flowers growing all year long. Three and a half dogs own her, two Shih Tzu lapdogs, a guardian Australian Shepherd, and the half a dog, a huge Labrador retriever who belongs to her son's family. The minute they leave home, the sociable lab visits grandmother. On holidays, the table swells with her daughter's family from the city. Everyone gathers for Jacquelyn Cook's Old South meals, especially Virginia-baked ham and devil's food cake with mocha frosting.